SLEWFOOT SALLY AND THE FLYING MULE

SLEWFOOT SALLY AND THE FLYING MULE

Tall Tales from Cotton County, Texas

by

Ardath Mayhar

The Borgo Press
An Imprint of Wildside Press LLC

MMIX

CONTENTS

FOREWORD

This is an oddball compilation of family tales, actual events, and stories told to me by old timers in East Texas. Some are sheer make-believe (as with my Dad's story of the inflated flea). Others, like the Possum Cats story, really happened with my grandfather and his brothers. The boys who caught the giant catfish (which actually exist in the rivers in the swamp country) are probably my brother and I, who wandered my grandfather's farm without let or hindrance from our early youth. As demonstrated here, weird people and behavior are rampant in this neck of the woods.

—Ardath Mayhar,
Chireno, Texas
April 2007

ABOUT THE AUTHOR

The author of sixty-two books, more than forty of them published commercially, **ARDATH MAYHAR** began her career in the early eighties with science fiction novels from Doubleday and TSR. Atheneum published several of her young adult and children's novels. Changing focus, she wrote westerns (as **Frank Cannon**) and mountain man novels (as **John Killdeer**). Four prehistoric Indian books under her own name came out from Berkley. Historical western *High Mountain Winter* was published by Berkley Books under the byline **Frances Hurst**.

Recently she has been working with on-line publishers. *A Road of Stars* was her first original novel to appear in print-on-demand format. Many of her out-of-print titles are now available from e-publishers fictionwise.com and renebooks.com; with many other out-of-print and original novels now being reprinted in book form by Wildside Press.

Now in her seventies, Mayhar was widowed in 1999, after forty-one years of marriage, and has four grown sons. The bookshop she ran with her husband for fifteen years was closed after his death. She now works at home, writing short fiction and nonfiction, and doing book doctoring professionally. Her web pages can be found at:

w2.netdot.com/ardathm/
and
http://ofearna.us/books/mayhar.html

I.

SLEWFOOT SALLY AND THE FLYING MULE

"It ain't that we set out to grow crazy folks around here," said Solomon Peat. He paused to spit neatly into an empty snuff can and set the lid back on tightly. A real gentleman was Solomon, not given to messing up his surroundings with tobacco-spit.

"Just seems to be somethin' in the ground or in the water that makes this old county turn up peculiar people. Why, I could point you at a dozen, right here in Possum Creek, that do things you wouldn't believe. Not bad things, you understand, just things that ain't done the way anybody else in the whole entire world would ever think to do 'em." He stared about at the conglomeration of kids and passers-by who cluttered the porch of the general store.

Nobody raised any objection to his statement, so he went on. "You take Thomas Pendleton, for instance, who rigged up a windmill to milk his cow."

That roused a rustle of interest among the youngest of his listeners, and he settled back, grinning, into his hickory-splint chair. "True as Gospel! Got one of these here milking machines that one of the dairies got rid of when they all went to the automatic equipment. Thomas bought him a little decompressor and a gover'ment surplus generator, and he milked old Blue-Spot with his windmill, pretty as you please."

"Well, that's just a matter of figuring out and rigging up," said the young salesman, who had finished dickering with Mrs. Bragg inside the store and was drinking a soda-pop and cooling off as he perched on the edge of the porch. "Anybody who put his mind to it could do something like that."

"But could just anybody make a big old mule fly?" asked Sol. He quirked a bushy white eyebrow at the young man. "And would anybody in their right senses try to?"

The young fellow shook his head. "Of course not. A mule has

got his place in the scheme of things, and flying isn't on his agenda. Who could follow a plow behind a flying mule, anyway?"

"Well Slewfoot Sally managed pretty well with hers," said Solomon.

There was a stir of interest on the porch. Five small boys edged up, leaving their elderberry popguns in the dust under the chinaberry tree and perched on the porch at Sol's feet.

He shifted his quid of tobacco around to lubricate his mouth. He spat again into the snuff can, wiped his lips daintily on the back of his sleeve, and stared off into the distant treetops as if he could see that mule flying over them, right that minute.

"She was an odd gal, old Slewfoot Sally. Had her a little old farm, not much bigger than a bed quilt, up over to Bobcat Ridge. She raised corn on the high ground and sugar cane in the bottom-land, and if she needed cash she sold some eggs or a few chickens. Independent as a hog on ice was Sal.

"Her folks had farmed up there since way back in the Spanish grant days, and every generation had cut up that land into littler and littler batches, until she hadn't more than fifty acres to her name. That didn't mean that nobody came courtin', once she grew up, even if she did have the biggest feet and the sharpest nose in the county. A bit of land comes in handy, even for a footloose man, sometimes, but she wasn't a bit interested. She liked to farm, did Slewfoot, and she did every bit of work on that patch of ground from building fence to breakin' new ground.

"Sam was all the male she had time for, and that was that."

"Who was Sam?" asked the salesman, who was now leaning against a post in a comfortable position.

"Why, her mule, of course. Smartest mule ever raised in Cotton County. He could teach a young'un to plow better than anybody I ever seen, mule or man. You could talk to him, and he'd look you in the eye and you'd swear he understood every word you said. He'd try anything Sal asked him to do, though he wasn't too fond of swimmin' with her in the creek.

"I've seen that critter follow her into the fields, come fall, and point birds as neat as any setter you ever did see. He wasn't much good as a retriever, though...he was too far up to see the killed birds down in the grass, and he either stepped on 'em or mashed 'em up a little when he picked 'em up to fetch."

The salesman choked on his soda-pop. When he got his breath, he waved both hands protestingly. "Now that's too much to swallow. I never heard of anything so ridiculous!"

"Ridic'lus or not, Sam was a pretty good bird-dog, or bird-mule might be a better way to put it. And a lot of other things, too, though anything needing hands was pretty well beyond him." Sol looked about as if quelling any doubts in his audience.

"But his best trick ever was when Slewfoot Sally teached him to fly." Again he glared about him, daring anybody to dispute his statement.

"That crazy woman taken it into her head that she wanted to learn to fly. Tried to take lessons down at the shirt-tail airport at Cottonwood, but they wanted more money than she could come up with. So she decided that if Sam could hunt birds and help her in the garden, he could fly, too. She was no fool...no way! She knowed it was going to take a lot of work to persuade that mule he could do such a thing, but nobody ever said Sal wasn't determined.

"She set him down in that shady front yard of hers and got right up close to his face and talked and talked and talked. I was there one mornin', delivering seed corn for Mrs. Bragg, and it was the beat-ingest thing I ever did see, the way that mule took in what she was saying."

"And what exactly was she saying that could persuade a mule that he could fly?" asked the salesman, in a sarcastic tone.

"Why she was telling Sam he didn't weigh hardly nothing at all. He could just walk right on up into the sky, if he put his mind to it. Take a load off his feet, too, she told him, if he'd start thinking the right way. They could go sailing around the country, seein' what folks was up to. Wouldn't need a car or truck that way, and they wouldn't have to buy gasoline.

"Besides, she told him, no mule had ever done it before. He'd be the very first flyin' mule in all history and he'd go down in the books that way, too. I could tell she was gettin' him all interested and enthusiastic, just by the way he twitched his ears and switched his tail." Solomon sighed deeply.

"I didn't believe she could do it, of course. I admit that right up front. I oughtn't to get riled at you all for disbelieving it, because I was the very first one to do that. I left, laughing to myself over that fool woman and her crazy notion. Next time I went up there was six months later. I needed to cut some firewood off Old Man Grogan's place, and I stopped, passing by Sal's.

"When I called, there seemed to be nobody home, though her old pickup was sitting under the elm tree. It looked like it had breathed its last, I tell you...grass was growed up all through the engine. I called, though, just to see if she might be out back some-place."

He stared around him, his bright blue eyes wide beneath the cottony brows. "And damned if Sam didn't come swooping right down and land in the front yard, neat as a pin. Sal was ridin' him, and her hair was all blowed everwhichaways. She looked pink and excited, and that sharp nose of hers didn't show up near so bad.

"She was real glad somebody'd come around so she could show off her mule's new trick, and she showed me how he could lift right off the ground and float, or run and take off and zoom away over the trees.

"She wanted me to ride him, but somehow I wasn't quite up to that. I got to thinking that he might get second thoughts about what he was doing, and if he had any doubts then down he'd prob'ly come, kerplunk!"

Solomon sighed. "She rode him for years, all over the county, and, for all I know, all over the state. They kept getting unusual radar sightings, and the Air Force would send out investigators, but all Sam had to do was light down in a grass patch and start grazin' and nobody ever paid him no never mind a'tall. I guess having that flying mule was the best thing old Sal ever had in her life. She died a happy woman.

"Funny thing, though. After the funeral, her brothers went up there to see to her stuff. They couldn't find hide nor hair of that mule no place. Sam was gone, slick as a whistle. Never did find him, and nobody ever sighted any carcass that might have been him, either."

The salesman was staring at the sky above the pines. He had gone pale, and his empty pop bottle had dropped from his fingers with a soft thud. He swallowed once, twice, three times. When he found his voice, he asked in a faintish tone, "How old do mules live to be?"

"Oh, sometimes thirty or forty, if they're well took care of and happy," said Solomon.

"It can't be," said the salesman. He got up and wandered over to his Ford. "That was a buzzard. A big buzzard."

He got into the car and cranked her up. But Solomon's sharp old ears caught the words he muttered as he put it into gear.

"A buzzard with a long, hairy tail...."

And then he was gone in a cloud of dust. Solomon looked far up above the pine trees. A speck of black was almost out of sight.

Sol smiled and looked down at the wondering faces on the porch. "No, we've got some strange folks here in Cotton County," he said. "But since Slewfoot Sally died, they're not near as strange as they used to be."

II.

THE BACKFIRE

It was getting along into spring. Birds were nesting all over the place, and a pair of jays was quarrelling over the proper care of their brood in Mrs. Bragg's chinaberry tree.

Will Henry, Solomon Peat's most faithful listener, came out of the store with Chuck, his crony. They were sipping their inevitable strawberry soda pops. He looked up at a particularly raucous cry and frowned at the jays. Out of a hip pocket came an elderberry popgun. It was too early in the season, as yet, for green chinaberries, so he had a pocketful of rounded pebbles, in case he needed ammunition.

Will Henry stashed his bottle securely in the corner of the porch and aimed. He popped the nearest jay forcefully in the tail feathers, and the bird squawked hysterically as it rose amid a flapping of wings. Will Henry turned to Solomon, who was sitting in his usual chair, watching with a grin on his big face.

"Got him," said Will Henry, swaggering to the edge of the porch and perching on the dusty boards.

"You sure did. I hate jays...they're noisy and have bad manners, just like some folks I could name. Baby jays is all right for a while, but they grow up to be big 'uns, just like their folks. Buzzards, too." He looked over the pine trees, where a circle of black shapes was floating quietly round and round, on watch for anything that might die in the next hour or so.

Sol began to chuckle. More and more of his fat was involved, as the chuckle became a belly laugh. The hickory splint chair joggled dangerously, and Will Henry began to look interested.

"What's so funny?"

Solomon wiped his face on his blue bandana and put on his tale-telling expression. "You ever hear your folks talk about old Doctor Ballard?" he asked.

Will Henry shook his head, but Chuck chirked up. "I did. My Uncle Samuel is named after him...not my own uncle, but Pa's uncle. Dr. Ballard brought him into the world, Pa said when I asked him how come the old fellow was named Samuel Ballard Hackman, when I never knew anybody else with a Ballard in their name in the whole entire family."

Sol nodded. "He was the right age. Old Sam's nearing eighty, now, and that would make him one of Doc Ballard's kids, sure enough. He was the only doctor for forty miles around, and though there wasn't many folks in Cotton County then, they managed to keep him pretty busy, what with havin' babies and breakin' legs and shootin' each other purely by accident, or so they said."

Mrs. Bragg came out onto the porch and stared up the road. She turned and looked down the other way, toward the river and Sundown Swamp. She shook her head and went back into the store.

Sol shook his head. "Catfish man's late again. Poor fellow—I'll warn him when he comes not to rile her any more than she is already." He spat into his snuff can and got back to his tale.

"The old Doc was married to Miss Katie, who was neat and pretty and had a temper that wouldn't wait. He purely loved to devil that woman, just to see her catch fire and shoot sparks. Besides that, he was a practical joker." Sol's belly began to joggle again.

"One time he taken a jar of tadpoles with him when he went to take out the Pearson boy's tonsils. Course, the boy was scared to death, and not noticing much, and Doc managed to keep pullin' out tadpoles instead of tonsils till he had that kid so tickled he got the tonsils without so much as a squeak. Mrs. Pearson didn't appreciate it much, but that boy was his slave for life."

Will Henry and Chuck were grinning, now. They'd had their own tonsils out a couple of years ago, and the sterile misery of the hospital seemed a poor second best to the tadpole method of tonsillectomy.

"Then again, there was the time Abraham Sorrels finally let him take out his appendix. It'd been botherin' that boy for years, and finally it got so he walked half bent over, and he give in and let old Doc cut on him. When he come to, Doc had a jar right there by his bed. The appendix was in it, all right, and wrapped around it was a garter snake about eight inches long.

"Doc told him it was the snake wrapped around that appendix that had give him all the trouble for so long. Abe believed that for nigh a week, till Doc give in and let on it was just a joke. That boy sulked for a month."

Chuck seemed to feel that the Doc Ballard tales reflected well on him, being as his family was, in a way, connected. Will Henry had to puncture that smug look. He stared up at Sol.

"And nobody ever got to him, real good?" he asked.

Solomon Peat began chuckling again, sending waves of fat rippling all over his body. "Not the way you mean. But he did get his comeuppance. He surely did."

He settled back in his chair. "Back in those days, folks paid the doctor with what they had. Being as they seldom had money, they paid with pigs and eggs and fresh-baked bread and turnips, if that's all they could scrape up. Miss Katie was used to finding the buggy that Doc used for making his rounds loaded to the gunnels, when he got back, with everything from turnip greens to taters.

"Well, one morning about this time of year Doc was jogging along a dusty track of a road when he saw a big old buzzard get up out of the ditch and take off. It didn't fly clean away, just sort of circled, waiting for him to get out of her way.

"Now Doc had never seen a buzzard nest in his life. He figured this was the time to see one, if he ever was going to. He reined in his mare and got out and stepped over into the ditch. Sure enough, there was the nest, and it had a hatful of the biggest eggs he'd ever seen inside it. Not humongous like ostrich eggs, now, but like the very biggest hen eggs you can imagine.

"He thought right off about Miss Katie's setting hen, that was setting on some eggs right that minute. He thought about Miss Katie coming out to see her new chicks and being met by a batch of awkward, ugly buzzard babies and it just about tickled him to death. He scooped up them eggs and put 'em in his hat, real careful. Then he went on about his day's work, which was the usual run of babies and bull gorings and broke legs and arms." Solomon looked up as the catfish man's car pulled up at the store.

The old man made a crossways gesture, and the catfish man nodded and went into the store. His face looked particularly meek and mild; everybody knew Mrs. Bragg's moods. Nobody wanted to get on the wrong side of her when she was in the grip of one.

Sol waited until the fellow was inside. Then he went on, "Doc was a smart fellow, but he tended to be absent-minded. He clean forgot about the buzzard eggs for several days."

Will Henry's eyes got bright, and he began to quiver, very slightly, all over.

"He come down to breakfast one morning, about five days later, and lit into his scrambled eggs and bacon and biscuit. He was always a good eater, and Miss Katie liked to cook for him.

"Well, he was about through when she turned away from the dishpan and said, 'Sam, who paid you in those lovely eggs, last week? I swear, they're just the biggest, richest eggs I've ever seen in my life. I'd like to buy some...we're just about out of the ones they gave you.'"

"Doc quit chewing, real quiet-like. He looked down at the last little remains of egg on his plate and sort of choked. 'Where'd you find those eggs?' he asked Miss Katie.

"'Why, in your hat, under the seat of the buggy. Most a week ago, it was. You forgot to tell me, but I always check it out, when you get back. Who was it? I'd truly like to get some more.'

"Doc was quiet for a minute, as if he was thinkin' hard. Then he shook his head. 'I forget,' he said. 'So many folks pay me in produce.' He got up from the table and left the house. Once he got to the buggy, he leaned over and threw up his socks."

Will Henry and Chuck were leaning on each other, awash with giggles. Solomon's face was bright pink, his glasses fogged with tears of laughter.

"Sure enough, old Doc had been eatin' the buzzard eggs all week, just enjoying the life out of 'em, never recalling for a minute the joke he'd intended to pull on Miss Katie. It near killed him, he told my Daddy, but he never let on to Miss Katie, though he went back into the kitchen and accidentally dropped the rest of those eggs while he was gettin' him a glass of milk."

Will Henry sighed. "I guess even the best of 'em have something backfire, don't they?" he asked.

"From time to time, they do," said Solomon Peat, staring up at the circle of buzzards. "Which only goes to show you that there is justice in the world, after all."

III.

THE LAST CAMP MEETING
IN COTTON COUNTY

The Methodist preacher didn't really approve of Solomon Peat. Oh, he howdied him when he went into Mrs. Bragg's store after milk or bread or his newspaper, but he did it in such a way as to tell anybody with eyes and ears that he thought Sol was a damned liar.

Of course, Uncle Sol knew that. He was no fool, and he'd seen three generations of preachers come and go over at Memorial Methodist. Being a lapsed Baptist, Sol didn't think much of any of them and didn't waste his valuable stories on them. Not often.

Brother Stinson, however, was different. He kept sort of needling Sol when he passed him on the porch. "Still fictionalizing?" he'd ask, with a sneer in his voice. Or, "I see you've got another bunch of fish on your line."

Sol took it in good humor, the way he did everything, smiling and paying it no never mind. But when Stinson kept on and kept on, never letting up at all, Solomon Peat got a mite riled.

It's never a good idea to get on the bad side of somebody with a fertile imagination. Particularly, it's not a good idea to do it with one who's got the brightest small boys in the county solidly in his corner. That's where the Reverend Stinson made his worst mistake.

Although the idea of camp meetings had gone out with the advent of the automobile, fifty years before, the preacher got it into his head to revive the custom. "There's no reason why you can't go and worship the Lord in a Ford or a Chevy, just as well as could be done in a wagon behind a team," he kept saying to anybody who'd listen.

After a while, the idea kind of caught on, and some of the local folks got in touch with kin in different towns in the county, and the Methodists got really excited about bringing back a good old religious custom, with a hymn-singing and even a fiddling contest to go

18

along with it.

Naturally, that reminded Uncle Sol of things he'd heard about from years ago when his Daddy was a youngster. He told stories of folks getting stuck in the deep mud fording the creeks and coming to preaching all muddy and wet and cussing a blue streak. He told about preachers trying to yell above windstorms that were taking the brush arbor shelters off right over their heads. By the week of the camp meeting, he had a big audience every evening, when he settled onto the porch of the store.

That really made Brother Stinson angry, but there wasn't any good way he could see to shut the old man up, so he had to keep quiet about it. He got real cautious about needling Sol when he passed him, as if he might suspect that he'd put his foot in something that he would find it mighty sticky to pull it back out of.

The weather was cooperating just right. It was June, not too hot, as some Junes can be in East Texas, but not too rainy either. People had already begun coming to town for family visits, combining vacation trips with the get-together at the church.

Wednesday evening was so pretty you could eat it with a spoon. Sol was cocked back against the wall of the store on two chair legs, and Will Henry and his chums were lined up on the edge of the porch, already halfway done with bottles of strawberry pop, by the time the sun was halfway down in the west. Old Man Kountze had just hip-hopped away down the road toward his shanty, and Sol was staring after him, half way daydreaming.

"Uncle Sol, tell us another story about the old-time camp meetings," said Will Henry. He turned up the bottle for another slug of strawberry pop, and his fellows followed suit.

"Eh? Another one?" Sol began to grin. "I've been saving the very best of 'em all for tonight. Tomorrow folks will start to arrive in earnest, and the preaching will begin. So I kept this one for last."

He spat into his snuff can and put the top on. After setting it down under his chair, he tucked his thumbs into his belt and let his head lean back against the wall. He began to chuckle, and the boys felt giggles begin percolating through their own innards. When Uncle Sol laughed, you knew something really funny was on its way.

"Back when my Daddy was a tad, just about like Will Henry here, there wasn't many folks here in Cotton County. They had to come from a long way before there'd be enough to get together a real humdinger of a camp meeting. Some folks would travel in wagons for three days to make it, and when they got here there was the hell-firedest preachers ever accumulated to give 'em their money's worth."

The boys hitched closer over the dusty boards of the porch. Their eyes were bright, and their mouths were half open to let all the flavor of the story soak into them.

"They testified and they sang and they moaned and they shouted, and they got sanctified for four days. Every night, they'd put their little 'uns into the wagons, wrapped up in quilts to keep the mosquitoes from eatin' them alive, and let 'em sleep. And the last night of all, they done the same, but instead of the old folks crawling into the wagons to sleep at the end of meeting, they all started off for home. Some traveled for a while and then camped, and some kept going until they got home.

"When the sun rose the next morning, there was consternation from Possum Creek to Joshua's Fork, from Fiddler's Crossing to Patchwork Ford." Sol's voice was deep and sad, but his eyes were twinkling with laughter.

"But why, Uncle Sol?" That was, of course, Will Henry. He'd finished off his pop and was leaning forward, waiting for an answer.

"Because my Daddy and a bunch of his friends, being too big to put to bed and too little to stay still for the preaching, went out in the dark and swapped all them little bitty kids around until nobody in the whole entire congregation went home with the right batch. Everybody had the right amount, understand. But every family that waked up kids the next mornin' found itself looking square at young 'uns that belonged to somebody else.

"Some they knew, of course, if they were kin or fairly close neighbors, but the little tiny ones that couldn't talk yet, they just hadn't a clue about them. Everybody had to come clear back to town and get together around the brush arbor and sort out the mess."

"What happened to your Daddy?" asked Will Henry. "Did he get caught?"

"Well, there was some that suspected who'd done it, but there was a dozen young fellows it might have been, and nobody talked, and there was just no way to prove a thing. Daddy got his britches tanned by his Daddy, just on suspicion, and he deserved it, too, but his reputation didn't suffer a mite...not more than it had already suffered, anyway, for other things."

Five sets of wickedly bright eyes stared up at Solomon. A pair of wickedly bright eyes stared back down at them. Nobody said a word. Sol ordered more strawberry pop all around, and Will Henry gulped his absent-mindedly. Sol could see the wheels in his head turning.

The camp meeting in Cotton County would have been a howling success. Only the last night's work of unnamed scoundrels disrupted the celebration. It took something like two days to return all the infants, who had been left sleeping in a row in the church nursery, to their rightful parents. When a child was in the right crib, wrapped in the correct blanket and sound asleep, what parent would ever have thought to check to make sure it was the right baby?

The resulting brouhaha was a source of gossip and speculation for weeks and months, and more than one bitter argument resulted in permanent feuds. Names were suggested and discarded. Threats were made.

But nobody thought of Solomon Peat, sitting innocently on Mrs. Bragg's porch, or of Will Henry and his chums. And you'd better believe they didn't say one word.

And that's why it was the very last camp meeting ever held in Cotton County.

IV.

More Ways to Skin a Cat

It was the cool of the evening. Being a Saturday, the store was still open, and Mrs. Bragg was inside selling ice cream to a carload of high school kids. Solomon, leaned back against the wall of the porch in his special chair, was enjoying the fragrant breeze and listening to the voices of the spring peepers, just barely audible in their multitudes from the direction of the swamp.

Three small black boys and two white ones were sitting along the edge of the porch, drinking one last strawberry pop, compliments of Sol, who was a sucker for Will Henry and Chuck and their cronies, Tim and Lester and Fane. Old Mrs. Sanger was rocking in Mrs. Bragg's Lincoln rocker, waiting for her husband to finish rummaging through the nuts and bolts bin. And Ezra Hicks ambled up the road and paused to greet the porch-sitters.

"Mr. Sol," he said, plopping down beside the boys, "how do?"

"Older and meaner," sighed Solomon. "But otherwise all right. How's it go, down there in the swamp?"

Ezra shrugged, his thin shoulders hunching together. "Worse. A sight worse than it used to be, before the river done changed its course agin and cut through to the lake."

Sol glanced at Flossie Sanger, who frowned back at him, her gray eyes almost lost in the map of wrinkles that was her face.

"Too bad," the old man said. "Hate to hear that, Ezra. Sundown used to be a good place to live, if you liked catfish and pineywoods rooter pigs. Anything new?"

Ezra heaved a sigh and reached up to run knobbly fingers through his tight-curled hair. "We're goin' to leave, Mr. Sol. Can't stand it no more, no way. Arlie's just about fit to be tied, and so am I, if the truth be known. We've lived in Sundown all our lives, and we hate to give up the house and the garden spot and the good fishin', but it's got beyond bearin'."

"That critter's still down there, then." It wasn't a question.

Mrs. Sanger rose from her rocker as if propelled by a spring. "George!" she squeaked, hobbling down the steps into the dust under the chinaberry tree. "Come on here, George! We got to go right now!"

George Sanger moseyed out of the store, only the crackle and jingle of his bagful of bolts marking his approach. When he saw Ezra he nodded, and he even hurried a mite as he joined his wife and helped her into their ancient Plymouth.

Solomon stared after them, his gaze sad. Then he looked back at Ezra.

"Not another one!" he said. "You don't mean to say...."

The skinny man sighed and nodded, his mahogany face sad. "Nother 'un, sure enough. Makes two, now. We can't stand no more of this. Arlie's leavin', no matter what I do. She says she don't have kids just to have 'em et up in the swamp."

"I can see that. I certainly can," said Sol. "Seems a shame, too. You used to come out of there with the finest fish I ever did see. And your Pa, till he got lost and never come back, did too. Where you all going?"

"Up to Arlie's Grampa. He and the old lady need some help on the farm. Hate to go that way, but you got to do what you can. I'm a fisherman, not a farmer, but you got to keep body and soul together." Ezra stood, his back slumped, his whole stance dejected, and his dark eyes the picture of sadness. "Bye, Mr. Sol. I'll be seein' you."

He moved away into the deepening twilight, and all the small boys watched his back out of sight. Then they turned to Sol and Will Henry asked, "What's he talkin' about, Uncle Sol? Out in the swamp? Pa told me he'd tan my hide if I ever went past that lightning-struck gum tree, but he didn't say why."

The young ones crept onto the porch, and Solomon found himself looking down into a semicircle of boys. He spat into his snuff can and wiped his mouth on his sleeve. Then he began.

"Ever since I was a minnow like you boys, there's been folks fishing in the river, and goin' down through the swamp to get there. Those big loops of the river switch back and forth, when the big rains bring down silt and stop 'em up, and that leaves deep holes that are just about the best fishin' places in the world.

"One of those is so deep and so wide and so long that it's a real lake. All the fish and things that was in it when it got cut off from the river itself, just fed by the creeks runnin' into it and the swamp drainin' off the extra water, has been there for the past hundred years or so. Them that lived that long, that is.

"My grandpa told me about fishin' there when he was a boy. It was plumb full of catfish, he said, and big bass with mouths that could swallow a man's head and sun perch as big as dinner plates. He used to set nets across the lower end, and when an alligator or a big gar didn't tear it to pieces he would come in with enough fish to feed ever'body in that end of the county."

"That's Catfish Lake," piped up Tim, the largest of the little black boys. "My Pa's been fishin' there."

"You're right. Catfish Lake. The river made it, away back, and about the time Will Henry, here, was born the river began to unmake it. There come a big flood, and the water got out all over the river bottoms and flooded the swamp and changed things up considerable. When the water went down again, it'd begun to open a channel out of Catfish Lake back into the river. First time in a century that had been so."

He spat reflectively into the can and settled more comfortably in his chair. Its back screeched along the store's wall, and Mrs. Bragg yelled, "Watch my paint, Sol!"

The front legs of the chair thudded to the floor, and Sol grunted a wordless reply.

"Well, when the lake had a channel wore through, that connected it up to the river again a couple of years ago, fish and things that had been trapped in there for generations started wanderin' out of their old home and lookin' around for new places. That was when folks that live along the river and the ridges of solid land in the swamp started to find their nets tore entirely to flinders. That's when some of 'em realized they couldn't swim in the river no more, nor let their kids swim there, either."

"Alligators," said Will Henry wisely. "Pa's seen big ones down there."

"Well, there was always gators, to be sure. But that wasn't what took Ezra's little Mary Jane, two years ago come July fourth. They come tearin' into town—their old pickup was still runnin' then—with her all wrapped up in a sheet, but it was no sort of use. Doc Landers just shook his head, when he unfolded the cloth and saw where her legs had been." He looked so solemn and sad that the boys' eyes widened, and their own expressions went still.

"Then it was Tater Roberts's best coon dog."

The largest of the black boys nodded vigorously. That dog's reputation had survived him by years.

"Fool dog chased a coon out in the river. Went after it, of course. Something just reached up and swallowed that coon, whole and entire, and it took that dog for dessert. I watched that with my own eyes. Me and Tater used to hunt together considerable, till I give up huntin' down there.

"And then it just come one thing after another...folks and dogs and hogs and even boats come up missin' chunks of themselves, or just missin', period. They got the game warden down there. He said it was a a big gator and hunted all over, till he come up missin', too."

"And what was it?" breathed Will Henry, his eyes wide and glistening, even in the darkness of the porch.

"A catfish," said Solomon. "Must be the biggest damn catfish ever bred in any swamp in the world. Tater and me saw it, when it come up for his dog. Head as big as the sofy in the church parlor. Whiskers like snakes. Makes a sort of gurgly sound when he comes up to breathe. Oh, we saw him, and that's when Tater moved out to town and got to be a mechanic and I quit huntin or fishin' in the swamp."

Will Henry cocked his head and looked skeptical with every line of his silhouetted shape. "Never heard of no catfish that big."

"They've caught 'em in the Atchafalaya swamps that weigh three hundred pounds," said Sol. "And one got caught someplace jungly, here a while ago, that weighed in at six hundred and fifty pounds. Even in the bayous they've netted two hundred fifty-pounders, too. Old Grampa Catfish, down there in the river, could eat those for breakfast. These two eyes seen him. You couldn't lay him in a pickup truck, without his tail draggin' a long ways on the ground."

"But why hasn't somebody cotched him?" asked Fane, the smallest boy.

"With what?" asked the old man. "No net nor hook nor pole nor set-line in the whole entire world could hold him. And if, by chance, one did...who'd take him off the line or out of the net? It'd be like tryin' to handle a dad-blamed elephant!"

"They say there's more ways to skin a cat than just one," said Will Henry. "There's got to be a way."

"Well, don't you go tryin' to figure out one," Sol said, his tone sharp. "Grampa'd eat you for a snack and never know he'd done anything at all."

The voices of the peepers, which had grown louder as darkness fell, suddenly went silent. The quiet was a shock, after the din before it. In the chinaberry beside the porch, a screech owl let out his quivery cry, and Solomon shivered.

"What made 'em do that?" whispered Tim.

"I dunno. I don't want to know. But I suspect that Grampa's come up for air," said Solomon Peat. He spat again into his can and rose from his chair.

The boys rose, too, and stood in a huddle, staring into the darkness off toward the distant swamp. As Sol stumped down the steps and set off for home, the boys, with one accord, turned toward their homes and began to run as fast as boy-legs could travel.

There was nobody left to hear the faint echo of a wet gurgly noise from the direction of the swamp.

V.

THE ALLIGATOR'S TALE

The sun was making itself felt, even under the shelter of Mrs. Bragg's porch. The store's puny air conditioner was whining to itself inside, where customers straggled in and out after a loaf of bread or a gallon of milk, instead of driving twenty-two miles to Tompkins, where they could buy both much cheaper.

Solomon Peat held no brief for air conditioners. He'd wrestled East Texas summers hand-to-hand and hide-to-heat for almost seventy years, and he didn't intend to wimp out now. His mass of fat ran with sweat till it sometimes dripped like rain off his elbows and chin, but he hung in there, and those who wanted to hear his tales had, by force of circumstance, to remain out on the porch in the heat.

Will Henry and his crew didn't like being indoors, anyway. The shade of the chinaberry made the air feel cooler, and the dust beneath the tree was grateful to bare feet. The ripening chinaberries also made perfect ammunition for five elderberry popguns, which wrought havoc with the jaybird population and kept even the arrogant mockingbirds nervously alert.

It was the arrival of a pickup load of fishermen, fresh from the river, that brought the boys onto the porch. Alf Swindoll always caught something interesting, and his load of grinning companions looked entirely too smug to be empty-handed.

They'd already dressed out ten big catfish—eleven-pounders, at a guess. They had some bass whose mouths were big enough to hold Will Henry's head. And best of all they had an alligator.

Sol grunted to his feet and leaned over the pickup bed to stare at the thing. "Sort of small, ain't it?" he asked Alf.

"Well, we didn't go gator hunting. This one sort of come after our bait, and we blew him to Kingdom Come. We're goin' to donate the stuffed hide to the library."

Sol grunted again and returned laboriously to his hickory splint chair. "Nice gesture," he said. "I sure wish Yancey's Pa had done that with his. It's purely wasted down in that shed of his."

Alf, however, had disappeared into Mrs. Bragg's, after ice for his fish. Will Henry, of course, hadn't missed anything, including Sol's tone as he assessed the gator.

"Mr. Yancey's got a gator?" he asked.

Sol chuckled, making his rolls of fat ripple and the sweat trickle instead of drip. "Got what's left of one, after you get the hide off him," he said. "You go look down there, first chance you get. Then come back and I'll tell you how old Kip Yancey happened to kill him."

Will Henry looked at Chuck, who turned to Tim, Les, and Fane. Two white faces and three black ones lit with immediate purpose.

"That shed right close to the edge of the swamp?" asked Will Henry.

"Where he keeps the tractor, when he's working his cornfield," Sol said.

"We'll go right now."

"Hey, you boys will cook your brains!" Sol protested. "Wait till sundown, at least. Or...." he recognized indomitable purpose in their expressions. "...at least get your caps out from under the porch and put 'em on."

Five dusty caps came out of their hiding place and were dashed onto five impatient heads. Will Henry and his crew headed off down the road, bare feet puffing up dust as if a small herd of horses galloped along.

Sol watched them reach the cornfield and cut across the standing corn, taking care not to injure any of the plants. When the last head had disappeared among the rows, he went into the store and came out with a cold Coke. By the time he had nursed it along by sips and finished it off, he reckoned that they'd be back.

After a while, the five boys bounded out of the corn and galloped up the road again, dust flying at their heels. Even before they got near, Sol could hear their excited voices.

"What a whopper!"

"By Johnny Jingo, it's a monster!"

He grinned. It was a monster, indeed. He had seen it in action, and alive it had looked even bigger than it did stretched to its full fourteen feet along that shed wall. He settled himself for a comfortable afternoon of tale-telling, noting that a gaggle of customers was approaching. His audience would probably be considerable, before he was done.

Will Henry flopped onto the porch, his round face scarlet with heat and emotion. Tim and his little brothers couldn't turn red, but they were sweating profusely, and Chuck looked rather pale.

"Here, you, Will Henry! Go inside and get every one of you a bottle of pop. Can't have you fallin' out with the heat," said Sol. He dug into his pocket and came out with some quarters. "And take Chuck into the washroom and cool him down. He looks kind of peaky."

When the boys were settled again on the edge of the porch, they looked refreshed...and expectant. Sol spat into his snuff can and wiped his mouth daintily. He liked to build up suspense.

"So you want to know how come that there gator is hangin' on Yancey's shed wall," he said at last. Five heads bobbed agreement.

"I seen it happen," he said. "I was right there, johnny-on-the-spot, watchin' with all my might. I was just the right age to recall it all, too, being only about sixteen at the time. My Daddy and Kip Yancey was partnerin' in catfish and wild hogs, that year. It was during the Depression, and food was what you could find for your-self, being as there wasn't any money floatin' around to buy any-thing with."

Mrs. Sanger, who had paused before going inside the store, sighed, "Amen to that!" and went in.

"We got pretty tired of pineywoods rooter hogs and catfish and cornbread, back then, but it was a sight better than being in town, where you hadn't anything to fall back on. We kept nets out in the river and in the lake. We hunted the swamp for razorback hogs. We made squirrel and rabbit stew and dumplin's. We trapped coons and possums and even birds, and they all went into the pot. Daddy had three boys and two girls, and Yancey had so many kids he never even tried to count 'em. So it took a right smart of grub to keep 'em all from goin' hungry."

Will Henry had heard the same sort of tales from his grandfa-ther, and he began looking impatient. "But the gator!" he said.

"Why that gator got caught right in the middle of our efforts to stay alive and kickin'," said Solomon.

"We had a net we'd all took a hand in making and stretched across one end of Catfish Lake. We'd caught a lot of big fish al-ready, though we had to mend tears the gar made in it from time to time.

"Then one morning we got the boat into the water and rounded the island in the middle of the lake, and we could see the trees we'd hitched our net onto just shimmying like belly-dancers. The water in

29

the middle was boiling and heaving, and we knew we had something we didn't want."

"And it was the alligator!" said Will Henry, jumping the gun, as usual.

"No," said Solomon, "it was AN alligator, not THE alligator. It was about seven foot long, and it took all of us to get it unraveled from the net, once we shot it. We was some tired and wet and disgusted by the time that was done and the net patched together again. All our catch got loose, of course, while we were at that. Only the fact that gator tail is good eatin' comforted us a bit."

"So where did that humongous gator come from?" asked Will Henry.

"Well, we decided, Tom Yancey and me, to go out in the swamp and hunt for hogs. Kip and Daddy went along the river, doing the same. And Kip had a brand new trick. He'd learned to squeal just like a big old pineywoods rooter.

"Tom and me, we sloshed through the swamp, and we didn't see a thing. It's in the fall you can be sure to find the critters among the hickory trees, but in the summer you just ketch as ketch can. We made it all the way round to the river, and there we could see Kip, out on a little sand spit, just squealin' away like a stuck hog.

"He had his old rifle cradled in his arms, and he was hunkered down on one knee, watchin' the far bank. We was upstream a bit, and we could see, right almost at Kip's feet, a pair of gator eyes, all knobby and almost invisible as bubbles, starin' up at him.

"Gators like pigs, too, you know."

The boys let out a series of shuddering breaths. Mrs. Sanger had come out of the store and was standing beside Sol, fanning herself with the magazine she'd bought and looking reminiscent.

"Tom, he let out a yell. 'Look down, Pap! Look down and to your left!'"

"Kip quit squealin' and glanced up at us, kind of mad, and Tom pointed. And Kip looked down.

"That old gun of his kicked like a Missouri mule. It knocked him flat on his back on the spit, being as he wasn't balanced to go shootin' it off right then. But it got that gator right between his knobby little eyes and struck at an angle to break his spine.

"I've never in all my born days seen such a to-do, not even when that grampa catfish ate the coon and the dog. Even with its spine messed up, there's a lot of whip and wiggle left in a gator.

"Me and Tom swum the river like scat and got ropes and hayhooks, which we'd brought to help with the hogs we killed, which counted up to none, right then. We finally got the critter hauled up on the bank. He measured fourteen feet, stem to stern. We skinned him out, real neat, and filled the hide with sand till it dried out some.

"Kip got his uncle to tan it good, and he hung it up in that shed and looked at it from time to time, all the rest of his life. Said it kept him humble to see how near he'd come to bein' et for a hog.

"And we had meat. Did we have meat! We ate gator tail roasted and boiled and fried and stewed and frittered and everywhichaways meat can be fixed. We got sick and tired of gator tail, even if it is good meat. But a fourteen-foot gator amounts to a whole hell of a lot of meat, any way you slice it, and we sliced it a lot of ways, I can tell you. Even Yancey's kids all had their bellies full, for once."

"And he's still up there on the wall. Who put in the glass eyes?" asked Chuck, his voice hushed with awe.

"Oh, Tom said he'd look a lot better with eyes than without, and he got a pair of marbles he'd quit playin' with a while before and stuck 'em in to look real natural. Log rollers, they used to call 'em. They looked kind of blind, but they did seem sort of lifelike."

"I had some of that gator tail, Solomon," said Mrs. Sanger. "Kip and Sadie carried my Ma some of it to trade for field peas. We enjoyed it, too. Tasty meat. Tasty meat." She tucked her magazine under her arm and limped down the steps and off up the road toward her ancient car.

"Lots of people tasted that old gator. A many of 'ems gone, too. And he's still up there, staring out at the world through log-roller marble eyes. Kind of strange, don't it seem to you?" He stared down at Will Henry, who nodded solemnly.

The boys turned up their forgotten strawberry pop bottles and took long pulls. But they kept staring off across Yancey's cornfield toward the shed, where the immortal fourteen-foot gator still reigned supreme.

VI.

FIRST YOU HAVE A PLAN

Will Henry wasn't your run-of-the-mill Cotton County boy. For one thing, he read everything he could get his hands on. That went for every book from the manuals for repairing tractors to the Bible. Along the way, he had encountered a very strange and hard to understand book titled *Moby Dick*.

He hadn't understood all of it—or even much of it—but something about the book had kept him reading. The vision of that terrible white whale and its one-legged pursuer had intrigued him at the time and continued to come to mind ever since.

That was why Uncle Sol's tale of the Grampa Catfish in Sundown Swamp took such a hold on him. Even running home that night, with the specter of the child-eating fish pursuing him to his door, he was thinking all the time. If a man could kill a whale, then by golly he should be able to catch and kill a dad-blamed catfish.

His father had been reading the paper in the living room when he pounded up onto the porch and almost tore the screen door off its hinges getting inside. Will Henry stood there in the sticky spring heat and the grateful yellow glow of the reading lamp. His father's bald head shone with a damp glimmer, and the hedge of stiff straw-colored hair standing up around the edges of his scalp seemed unusually comforting and familiar.

"Pa?" the boy asked, his tone quieter than usual.

"Eh? Oh. Will Henry." Pat Emerson lowered his paper and looked inquiringly at his son.

"Did you ever hear tell about a humongous big catfish down in the river below Sundown?"

Pat's brow furrowed, all the way up to the crown of his head. He didn't believe in boogey-man tales to scare children.

"Well, yes. Heard something about it, but it didn't seem sensible, so I didn't believe it."

"You think Uncle Sol would lie about actually seein' it?" Will's voice trembled. He knew there were liars in the world. He even told a whopper himself, from time to time. But he had never doubted anything Uncle Sol told him, no matter how outrageous. He, too, had seen something flying over the pine trees that looked far more like a mule than a buzzard, from time to time. And he had seen Yancey's gator with his own two eyes.

His father laid the paper aside and put his hands on his knees. His bald spot was now wrinkled all the way back to the hedge of hair at the back. He shook his head slowly. "No. I'd trust Uncle Solomon about as far as anybody I know. He said he'd seen the thing? Himself?"

"Yessir. Him and Tater Roberts together, when they was hunting and it got the dog and the coon the dog was chasin'. Both. Uncle Sol said its mouth was as wide as the sofa in the church parlor."

Emerson sighed. True or not, he didn't want Will Henry frightened. The boy had too much imagination as it was, without adding monster catfish in the swamp.

"I didn't hear anything that clear and first hand. You just forget about it and go wash up for supper. You ain't allowed to go into Sundown, anyway. And don't forget that!" He stared over his glasses at Will Henry. "Hear me, boy?"

Will Henry nodded. That was no lie. He did hear. He didn't intend to obey, but he did hear it, loud and clear.

That night, he dreamed of a white catfish with a peg leg tied onto its belly. It chonked a bite out of Pa's flat-bottomed fishing boat and stared him in the eye as he sank into the murky water of the river. He woke sweating, wound up in the sheet like a mummy, with his heart thudding triple time in his damp chest.

That was when the idea came to him, full-blown and beautiful. He'd go on his own hunt, not for a whale but for the tremendous catfish that had lived for a hundred years and grown to such a size that it was no longer to be classified as a catfish at all. It was an elemental, a monster out of myth. And he was like Saint George...the very one to slay that monster and avenge poor little Mary Jane and Ezra's other lost child.

Once he had made that decision, Will Henry sank into a delicious sleep that lasted until his mother tugged off the sheet and spilled him onto the floor, her usual method of getting him up for school on a lazy spring morning. For once, he didn't dawdle and yawn and waste time getting dressed and eating his breakfast. He tore out toward the schoolhouse almost without any nagging at all, and when he got to the chain-link fence around the playground, he found Chuck huddled with the other three members of their special small and select brotherhood.

"Tim! Lester! Fane!" he greeted the brothers. "Chuck!" He turned toward the big pine tree beside the drinking fountain and sat on a root, which was gnarled from generations of small feet and bottoms. "I've got just the best idea I've ever had in my whole entire life!"

The four followed him and sat, their eyes bright with anticipation. When Will Henry had an idea, the world seemed to brighten up all at once, and things tended to get lively.

"We're going to catch that Grampa Catfish down in the river," he said.

They flinched backward. Not one of them had failed to feel the threat of that monstrous fish that had eaten children and boats and probably at least one game warden, uniform and all. The ringing of the bell was the only thing that prevented an outcry of protest.

Will Henry hadn't counted on the reluctance of his henchmen. He spent history class thinking of good arguments, which netted him a "D" in a subject he knew perfectly, for he couldn't keep his mind on the pop test. He did as much figuring on his plan as he did on his arithmetic, which resulted in a "B," whereas he usually made an "A" for classroom participation.

By the time noon rolled around, he had things sorted out. He found Chuck saving him a place in the cafeteria line, as usual, and he slid in behind Fane and his brothers.

"Just you wait until after lunch! You're going to love this plan," he said. The teacher shushed him from farther along the line, and he could only nod emphatically when one of his cronies looked around at him.

They got through eating in record time. Then they settled onto the pine tree roots expectantly, and he marshaled his arguments one last time before beginning his spiel. It still sounded good.

"This is prob'ly the last really big adventure left, if you don't intend to be an astronaut or something like that," he began. "How many dragons are there left for folks to kill? Wars are old hat, and besides they never were as big a deal as they were cracked up to be. Shit, we could live to be old men and never come up with such a chance again." He gazed around, but his audience still looked skeptical.

"When we get that critter in our hands, we can make folks PAY to see him. Fact is, we can sell enough meat off him to give each of us a nice amount, and then we can pickle his bones somehow and keep chargin', if anybody still wants to see them. Why, I bet even the TV people might be interested."

That brought a gleam into every pair of eyes. To be on TV was the secret dream of every one of them. The glamour of that took their breath away.

"And more than that, I'll bet you anything that there's never been another catfish that big. We could prob'ly get in *The Guinness Book of World Records*!"

He had them. There wasn't one of them who didn't have, somewhere among his possessions, a dog-eared and well thumbed copy of one of those books, *The Guinness Book of World Records*.

Tim looked a bit dazed at the magnificence of the possibility. His down-to-earth character, however, demanded some solid evidence that the thing could be done. "And how do we go about catchin' that monster?" he asked.

Will Henry had given that some thought, too, while failing his history test.

"Why, we'll ask Uncle Sol. He knows just about everything.

"But we're not going to tell him what we're planning. We're just going to talk about fishing. It's spring. Everybody goes fishing in the springtime. Everybody goes after the biggest fish they can catch, too, so we're going to ask him about how to get the whoppers in Denman's Slough. I figure anything that will hold one of those will be worth considering, if we can figure a way to double or triple it."

"There's poisons for fish," whispered Fane. "I heard my cousin Donny talk about how he got fined for using one, once. He got a catch of white perch and sun perch and gar and drum...washtubs full, he said. But he got caught and the game warden taken it all down to the old folks home."

Will Henry took his little spiral notebook out of his pocket, along with his pencil stub. "Poison," he said, noting it. "That's a good beginning. Good work, Fane."

Les, not to be outdone, piped up with, "What about telephonin' for fish? I heard my grandpa talk about it, once, but I don't ezactly know what he meant. Somethin' about an old-timey phone with a handle you crank that makes electricity go in the water. Sounded funny to me, but he swore it worked."

"We'll ask Uncle Sol," said Will Henry, adding 'phone' to his list. "That'll just come up natural, if you ask him what your grandpa meant by it."

"Rotenone," said Chuck. "That's one of the poisons. I heard my dad mention it once. And then that was what they used in *The Creature from the Black Lagoon*...you 'member the movie we saw on TV? It's sort of a white powder, I think."

Will Henry smiled. "See how easy it's going to be? We're going great guns, now. Be thinking about anything else you ever heard about ways to get fish, besides with a pole and line."

The bell rang. He put his notebook back into his pocket and stood.

"We're going to get us a catfish, fellows, but first we got to have a foolproof plan!"

VII.

To Capture Leviathan

"Uncle Sol?" Will Henry managed to sound completely inno-cent.

Solomon Peat, leaning against the wall of Mrs. Bragg's store in his chair, jerked from his doze. The spring morning was already very warm, and the shade of the porch lent itself to dozing.

"Les's grandpa told him a tale about telephoning for fish. Used one of those old-timers like Miss Hooks has in the library for show. Was he telling a whopper, or was it for real?"

Sol smiled his slow grin, which still held more than a bit of a boy's wickedness among the wrinkles that now surrounded it. He let the chair's front legs down onto the floor with a soft thud and leaned forward, elbows on knees.

"Now that brings back some memories. Yes, it does, indeed," he said.

Will Henry scrunched closer, followed by Chuck, Les, Tim, and Fane. "You've done it?" he asked, his tone incredulous.

Sol looked offended. "You think there's any mischief invented in this county in the past fifty years or more that I ain't been into?" he asked. "Telephonin' for fish is strictly illegal, remember that. I ought to have been whipped for goin' along with it. Come to think of it, I was whipped, in one way, and deserved it, too, which wasn't always the case." He glared at the boys.

"But nevertheless, I went one time and once only to try that method of catchin' fish. It was s'posed to be the most efficient way ever devised for gettin' 'em without killin' 'em. My brother Yale, who was years older than me, and his friend Caz, and our little brother William, that you was partly named for, we decided that we was going to make the biggest haul of fish ever took from the river." He spat neatly into his snuff can and stared off across the pines as if he could see those young fellows, right that minute.

"We picked the middle of the summer, when the river was dried up in the shallows and only had deep holes of water standin' where eddies had filled the loops. The fish was hungry, and it wasn't no big trouble to catch all you wanted with a line and pole, but we wanted to try this newfangled way.

"We borrowed Uncle Tom Batcheler's phone out of his back shed, where it was waiting to get put into his new house. We figured it might as well be doin' somebody some good, while it was waiting to be used. It was a big old wooden box, bigger than the one they've got in the library, with a crank handle you could really get a grip on, which it turned out was a very good thing. It's a sight easier to talk about telephonin' for fish than it is to do it."

"Why?" demanded Chuck.

Sol chuckled. "You can twirl that little handle just as easy as pie, long as it ain't really havin' to generate much juice. We tried it, after we got down to the hole we'd chose for our experiment. Nothin' to it. Then Yale dropped the wire we'd put onto the little generator into the water. Wowee!" He chuckled all over, his belly quivering, his jowls shaking. "It was like all of a sudden that handle was set in concrete. I couldn't turn it at all. Caz could just barely make it turn a little bit. It took Yale, who was a big cuss and strong as two mules, to spin it fast enough to put any juice at all into that water."

Will Henry was all but quivering with curiosity. "But what did you catch?" he asked, his tone betraying his intense interest.

"Just about everything," said Solomon. "You never seen so many fish come floatin' to the surface. Little ones come first, sun perch and minnows and little catfish and young bass and carp and all kinds of trash fish. Then the bigger ones began to come...not dead, mind you, but stunned. We ignored the little ones. We could catch those by the bucketful, when we had a mind to. But when the two and three-pounders began coming up, though, we waded in and started picking out the very best for our real catch."

Mrs. Bragg came out of the store and stared off down the dusty road. "Solomon, you keep an eye out for the bread man. I'm about to run out, and he's late." She turned and stumped back into the store, her square back daring him to argue with her.

"Now how does that woman think that my keepin' an eye on the road is going to make that salesman come a bit quicker than he'll come anyway?" asked Sol, of nobody in particular.

He hitched his chair around so that his back was toward town. He didn't argue with Mrs. Bragg, but he never did what she told him to, either. Not often, anyway.

Will Henry was bouncing up and down on his skinny bottom. "Tell about what all you caught!" he said, squirming impatiently.

"When the really BIG ones started rising, we got sort of scared. We hadn't known there was stuff in that river that was most as long as we were. We pulled out a catfish that would've weighed about ninety pounds, I expect, though we had no way to tell exactly. It was a lot heavier than William and most as heavy as me. We put him in the wagon we'd borrowed from Caz's Daddy for our fishing trip, and we was all puffed up, we was so proud. Still, it was spooky to think that we'd been swimming all summer over the heads of critters that could have just about swallowed us with one chomp."

The five boys were sitting in a semicircle, now, flat on the porch, legs curled beneath them, eyes wide in their grimy, tanned faces. "Wow!' said Les softly.

"We got a bass that had to weigh five pounds. It was a monster, though of course not near so big as that cat. Then, when we had the surface of that hole literally covered with great big fish, just asking to be hauled in, that damn gar come up. And he was a sockdolager."

The boys nodded with understanding. Every one of them had seen the big alligator gar that lived in the river. Every one had come across the huge dead bodies on the banks, where they'd been caught in fishermen's nets and hauled out and killed. Once Will Henry had taken an axe to an especially big one, but he hadn't done anything but dull a good axe and knock off a few arrowhead-like scales.

"That sucker was eight feet long. We hauled him out and tied knots in a length of line to measure him, and when we got back home we measured it with Caz's Daddy's folding rule. Eight feet and three inches and a quarter, to be exact. He weighed a ton.

"We couldn't get him into the wagon, no way. Not that we could've used him, we just wanted folks to see a really BIG gar, for once in their lives. We planned to sashay right through town with our wagonload of whoppers and startle everybody into the middle of next week." He spat again, wiped his mouth, and sighed.

"Well of course we couldn't load him, and we was too lazy to haul him off to one side of the wagon, so we just let him lay. Didn't think once that those critters are born tough and the electricity might wear off him sooner than any of the others. So when Yale stepped up to put a nice white perch the size of an iron skillet into the wagon, he was some surprised to feel them big narrow jaws with all their dozens of teeth chonk down onto his ankle."

"It bit him?" That was Tim, his eyes wide so that the whites showed all around.

"Bit him? It got him fair and square, and not a thing we could do would make him let go. There was Yale yelling and using some language I never told Mama he knew, and me and Caz and William beatin' on that fish with rocks and sticks and trying to prize its jaws loose, and not a bit of it doing any good at all. The whole thing together was sure as hell too heavy to lift into the wagon, with just three of us, and we was just about to decide that Yale was a goner when William had an idea."

Chuck bounced, his bony butt tapping on the boards of the porch. He didn't ask, but his eyes were wide.

"William went and got that telephone out of the wagon. He put the wire down into the gar's mouth, sliding it between Yale's shin and the corner of the jaw. Then he looked at me.

"'You and Caz got to work the damn thing,'" he said. 'You know I can't turn it.'

"Well, we set up that box and I held it and Caz grabbed that handle and fairly made it fly. It wasn't near so hard sending juice into that gar as it had been gettin' it to go into the water. The gar give a jerk and a flip, and Yale was free and the gar was flopping his way back to the water. We let him go. We let the rest of 'em go, too."

"Even the ninety-pound catfish?" Will Henry sounded unbelieving.

"Even him. We felt, somehow, that maybe we'd been doing somethin' that wasn't really right. We knowed it was illegal all the time, but there's lots of things that's illegal and still aren't wrong, if you think about it pretty hard. This had begun to feel wrong.

"Yale, in particular, knowed something he'd never thought of before, and that was how it felt to get caught by somethin' bigger and stronger than you are. He didn't like that feeling a bit, and he saw to it that every last minnow was put back in the water. We watched till they all livened up and darted back down into the deep water." Sol sighed.

"Then we went home. Went by and put Caz's Daddy's wagon in the shed. Put Uncle Tom's telephone back in its shed, after wiping off most of the mud and dead leaves and stuff that was sticking to it. Far as I ever heard tell, it worked just fine, once he got it in the house.

"Our folks asked why we was back so quick, and Yale showed his leg and said he'd got hung up in barb-wire, which was what it looked like, sure enough, if you didn't look close enough to see the tooth marks.

"We cleaned up and sat around in the back yard, pretty quiet, and after a while we went to bed. I, for one, was mighty glad we was all there, safe and sound, and I made up my mind that if anybody was going to telephone for fish again, it sure as hell wasn't going to be me."

The boys rose from the porch. They looked satisfied. Will Henry said, "Thanks for the pop, Uncle Sol. And the story. That was something we really and truly wanted to know about."

The boys filed away down the path into the spring day. Miss Hooks would never know how nearly her antique telephone had come to being abducted for nefarious purposes, which was just as well for all concerned.

VIII.

Milton Peake and Nephew

Will Henry, Chuck, and Tim decided, one Saturday morning, to reconnoiter Sundown Swamp and its environs between the river and Catfish Lake. "If we know what's there, it won't be so worrying trying to figure out how far we're going to have to go and what all we'll need when we get there," the Fearless Leader said.

That seemed reasonable, though every one of them was forbidden to go near the swamp without an adult at hand. The bigger boys left the smaller ones fretting in the shade of Mrs. Bragg's chinaberry tree very early one late spring morning, hiking out for the swamp before Solomon Peat had even made his appearance. The fewer awkward questions, they felt, the better.

The three trotted across Mr. Yancey's field, where the young corn was now hip-high, and found themselves in the hem of the dense forest edging the swamp. They got there rather more quickly than they expected, and it was still dark beneath the towering hickories and sweet gums and even darker, once they entered the swamp, under the cypresses.

There was, to Will Henry's surprise, a well worn path leading into the swamp. Its surface, so late in the season, was already dusty, and the tracks of possums and raccoons and muskrats and birds of all kinds patterned it. Feeling encouraged, the boys went single-file along the twisting route, following its series of connecting ridges and hummocks in a shortcut that took them at last to the banks of Catfish Lake.

Not one of them was old enough, as yet, to have gone there with one of the fishing expeditions their fathers made at least once a year. The lake lay in a fishhook curve, its farther reaches lost behind a small island in the middle. Will Henry dropped to his knees in the trail.

He began sketching in the dust. "Now here's the lake...see this loop. And here, between the lake and the river, is the swamp. Somewhere along there has to be the new channel, but the lake sure enough doesn't look as if it has lost much water, does it? If we go along that way...." He sketched a line toward the east.... "We'll get to the river. Old Grampa Catfish will be there, I reckon."

Tim grunted. "You s'pose he ever comes back up that new channel to see his old home? Maybe he got kinfolks in this lake."

Chuck snorted. "That flood that took the channel back out was a big 'un. Prob'ly washed him with it, and now the channel might be too shallow to let him back in."

Nevertheless, he looked sideways at the lake and jumped when a big bass struck at a damsel-fly that had been flittering along just above the water.

They struck off along the track. Map or no, they had to go where the dry land led or sink to their chins in the ooze alongside. After a while, they came to a wide break in the low ridge. Before them lay the channel, its waters swirling lazily with the slackened flow of the season.

A moccasin was curled into a button willow bush in the shallow water. It raised its wicked little head to watch them pass. A middle-sized frog gave a hysterical yelp right under Chuck's feet and leaped into the water. Chuck almost followed it, but Will Henry caught his arm in time to haul him back.

As they stood staring into the water, they became aware that they were, in turn, being stared at. Will Henry pointed downward, silent for once. A pair of knobby eyes protruded from the water. In the whiskey-colored water of the channel lay a long body, submerged and unobtrusive.

"If you hadn't of caught me, I'd of been eaten for sure," said Chuck to his friend, his voice trembling. "That gator is just waiting for his chance."

They were gulping and staring when there came the thud of a footstep. They felt it quite plainly through the soles of their sneakers. The eyes disappeared as silently as if they had never existed, and the long body seemed to evaporate before their gazes.

Will Henry looked around and found himself staring rudely at two people coming through the tangle of cattails and grass and willows and briar vines that edged the swamp. When they stepped out onto the track, he saw that they were as barefoot as geese, too, which in moccasin country seemed pretty short-sighted.

"Good morning," said the older of the young men. He looked pretty old, once you studied him a bit...all of thirty or thereabouts.

His companion was dirty and ragged and fagged-out looking, but he couldn't have been more than sixteen or seventeen, Will Henry thought.

"Morning," said Will Henry. "You folks got lines out?"

The man laughed softly. "Lines and traps, too. We live down here. At least for the time being."

The notion staggered Will Henry. He'd never heard of anybody living right in the swamp without having a house on stilts and a boat. These fellows didn't seem to have much of anything but themselves.

"I'm Will Henry Emerson," he said. He put out his hand in the grownup way he admired so much.

"Milton Peake," said the man. "And this is my nephew Fred. He's the reason we're here. You, Fred, go run the trap we set over yonder. And don't step on any snake without catchin' it. A moccasin is as good eatin' as a rabbit, any day."

Will Henry felt something hot rise into his throat. He controlled it, however, and hunkered down beside the man. He didn't quite know how to ask the questions that were boiling up inside him without defying the manners his Mama drummed into him every day of his life. Before he could think of the right question, the man spoke.

"Nossir, never thought I'd come over here to Sundown. I had a good job working the oil rigs. Made a lot of money. It's still in the bank, pilin' up interest. Once Ma died and I left this neck of the woods, I never intended on coming back, but when Sis called to tell me her boy was in trouble with the law—for STEALIN'!—well, I just quit my job and hot-footed it back to see what I could do." He sighed.

"Fred...stole?" asked Will Henry. He'd never met a thief, at least not one that had been caught and identified as such, and he thought it was a very interesting thing to find in the middle of the swamp.

"Fred was a thief," said Milton. "When he gets the last of that foolishness out of his system, we'll go back to town and he'll go back to his Mama. Until all the shit gets driven out of him, by God, we're going to stay down here and live in the hollow magnolia and eat what we can catch.

"Now and again, the lawyer comes down to see how he's doing. He's got custody or whatever they call it. Every time he does, that fool boy just begs and pleads to be took off to jail. No way we're goin' to let him off as easy as that. He's goin' to sweat it out in the swamp, if it takes us another winter."

"You were down here all winter?" asked Tim, in an awed tone. "It got pretty cold, last winter. You didn't get sick?"

"When you live in the swamp, you get too tough to get sick. 'Sides, you ketch things from people, not from frogs and fish and alligators. We got along just fine. Slept cold, of course, but that's good for Fred. He'll appreciate a bed, time he gets into one again."

"But how did you know how to live down here? Even the folks that was raised here can't get along the way you do," said Chuck.

Peake stared off into the tangle of waterweeds and willows and cypresses. "I was raised in a place just like this, over on the Nicha-yac. They've ruined all that, now, which is why I come to Sundown. My Ma was left to raise all us kids, and I trapped and fished and we made it fine without ever touchin' a nickel of welfare money. You'd better believe that I know all there is about livin' off the land or the swamp, as the case may be."

Will Henry sighed, long and drawn-out. Such a romantic tale hadn't come his way in a while, despite Uncle Sol's efforts.

"Takes a good man to put hisself out so much for his kinfolks," he said. He didn't recognize it, but his very tone and words might well have come out of his father. "Not many would, I reckon. You think old Fred's doing any good?"

"I think he's most cured," said Peake. He rose and grinned down at Will Henry. "What you all doing down here, anyway? I'd think your folks wouldn't let you come so far in by yourselves. I know this old swamp and lake and river from end to end, now, and I can tackle a gator and give him the first bite, but you all ain't quite big enough yet to do that. There's things would eat you for a snack and then look around for the main course."

Will Henry chuckled. "My Pa told me not to come," he said. "He's a good man and a good Pa, but I just can't stand to be told not to do somethin'. It makes my belly ache."

This was, of course, not quite the entire truth, but he thought Milton would accept it. There was something in the fellow's expression that said he wasn't too good at taking orders, himself.

Milton laughed aloud. "I done the same, in my time, when Ma got too worrisome about things. Won't harm you, if you're careful. But don't go swimmin' in the river. There's a catfish out there big enough to give a elephant a hard time."

Chuck managed to say, "We got no intention of goin' swimmin' anyplace. We just wanted to knock around and see if we could find some good fishing holes."

Peake nodded, three abrupt jerks of his head. "Course you want that. Every boy I ever knowed wanted the same. You fish in this channel, boys, and I bet you'll come up with more fish than you can shake a stick at. Not great big ones, but they're a pain to carry out from this far, anyway. Good luck to you."

He raised a hand to Fred, who had emerged from a fringe of willow trees and was hauling along a stringer of catfish that would have bugged the eyes of any fisherman in Cotton County. Tied around the neck at the end of the stringer was a big fat water moccasin. It wasn't entirely dead, as the squirming of its tail indicated, but there wasn't a thing it could do about its present predicament.

As the pair moved away, sharing the weight of the stringer between them, Will Henry decided that he was mortally grateful he wasn't the one who had to take that moccasin loose. Adventure was one thing. Snakes were altogether different.

"Well, we found out what we wanted to know," said Tim.

Will Henry came out of his daze. "We did?"

"Why sure. We know that catfish is out in the river. Prob'ly ranges up and down where the channel goes out. My grampa says big fish likes to get near an outflow and just set there and gobble up the little 'uns that's carried with the stream."

"By golly, you're right," said Will Henry. Chuck nodded agreement.

"That means we'll have time to go back to the store and see if Uncle Sol'll buy us a strawberry pop."

There was no disagreement. They would never have admitted it, but the hugeness of the swamp, the gator, and that squirming moccasin, not to mention the words of Milton Peake, had made them feel a bit shivery and cautious.

"We'll catch him, of course," said Will Henry, as they emerged into Yancey's cornfield. The other two nodded. It was going to take a bit more than they'd thought to accomplish that, however, and all three of them knew it.

IX.

THE DULLSHOOTER

Popguns made from elderberry shoots and loaded with green chinaberries were all very well for the boys of Possum Creek, but every boy in Cotton County wanted a B-B gun. Their fathers were farmers and loggers and fishermen, however, and money was not plentiful.

When Will Henry's Uncle Stafford Emerson, who was a school-teacher up in north Texas, sent the boy a B-B gun for his birthday, he was the envy of all his peers and quite a few of his seniors. Even Solomon Peat looked a bit green.

The boys were under Mrs. Bragg's chinaberry tree, having set up a cardboard box as a target. Each was taking a turn with the gun, Will Henry doing the refereeing, and squabbles were inevitable.

Solomon leaned back in his hickory splint chair and gazed long-ingly at the sharpshooters. He would have given a lot to be ten again, taking his turn with the shiny new gun.

"Going to make sharpshooters out of the whole entire bunch," said Benny Long, who was perched on the edge of the porch. His tone was wistful.

"It don't always work," said Sol, spitting into his snuff can. "I've seen it fail just miserable."

"They say practice makes perfect!" protested Benny.

"Some folks can practice till Doomsday and it don't do one bit of good," said Sol. "Like José Morales. He spent a good bit of his life shootin' at one thing or another. He was in the Army and landed on a whole bunch of them little old islands out in the Pacific Ocean, durin' the war. I shiver to think how many of his own folks he must have killed by accident. No, old José just couldn't hit the side of a barn...even if he was on the inside of it!"

Benny twisted around to find a comfortable position, for Sol's voice had taken on its storytelling tone. The domino players on the other end of the porch cocked their ears, and the shuffle and click of the dominoes slowed down considerably.

"José Morales's folks come here long before any of ours did," he began. "There was Moraleses settled in Cotton County before it ever had a name, much less any Anglos. They was kin to the King of Spain, I've heard it said, though they never was a bit stuck up about it. Me'n José went to school together, and I got to know him pretty well.

"He was a shy kind of fellow, but he had a real good heart. He hated it when he got drafted and sent off to train for the War. I got sent to Kansas, so I didn't know how he come out till we both was back here at home." He spat neatly and gazed at the boys under the tree. The spitting sound of the B-B gun brought him out of his reverie.

"He was in a lot of action. Went ashore on Guadalcanal, on Truk...just all over. Said he tried not to shoot that gun they give him, 'cause it was plain and simple, right off, that he couldn't hit a damn thing with it. He was scared to death he might blow some of his buddies to Kingdom Come. But nobody listened to him, and he kept wading ashore off them landing craft and up onto islands where bullets was zinging around like bees in the spring.

"I thought he had to be exaggeratin', so I got him to come out to the house—that was when I lived down in the cabin across the river—and taken him out for target practice. Then I believed him, sure enough. He could aim at an oak and hit an elm, every last time.

"He always hit somethin', but it never was what he was aimin' at...it was like the gun had a will of its own, so to speak. And I couldn't see one damn thing wrong with the way he aimed or stood or sighted. Looked as if he ought to knock the eye out of a gnat."

"Well, not everybody's cut out to be a sharpshooter," said Benny.

"That's true enough. And José was cut out to be a dullshooter, if anybody ever was. Out where he settled with his wife and kids, that was a real handicap, too. There's still varmints back in the woods that will eat your chickens and even your calves, if you're not on your toes. Back then, it was a sight worse.

"José kept his pa's old thirty-ought-six loaded. His Maria was a crack shot, and she used to keep the possums and the hawks and bobcats off their poultry and stock mighty well. But she had to go off and tend to her Ma, when the old lady got sick with her final illness, and that left José there with the little kids and the varmints and that big old gun. Made me nervous just to think about it."

Will Henry's voice shrilled, "Now if you don't want to do like I say and shoot by turns, you just don't want to shoot this here gun at all, now do you? I'll just pack it back in the box and take it home, and we can play with popguns. I don't like fussing and fighting."

Solomon smiled.

"Who'd he shoot?" asked Benny, whose people had moved into the county only twenty years before. He was still a newcomer, by anybody's standards.

"Well, not a who. But not what he intended to hit, either. About a week after Maria left for her Ma's, he heard a racket out in the cow pen that brought him straight up in bed. They had a new calf, and it wasn't safe to let the cow and calf out to graze at night, so they kep' 'em in the lot.

"When José heard the cow bawling and the calf raisin' sand, he knowed something was after that calf. He jumped into his pants and boots and got that rifle out of the corner where Maria kept it, and off he went to save his livestock." Sol began to laugh.

He wiped his eyes and sighed. "It really ain't funny, of course. I didn't laugh a bit when José told me about it, but afterward I got off in a private spot in the woods and just whooped. It was just so much like José.

"He got there with his lantern and hung it on a stob so he could see to shoot, and there in the middle of the cow lot was a cougar big as all outdoors. It had been after the calf, of course, and he upped with the thirty-ought-six and let her rip.

"The cougar was gone like a streak, and never a hair nor a drop of blood could he find. He missed it clean, but he killed that calf, way off in the corner, dead as a doorknob. It was almost behind him, he swore, and all the way out of the direction he shot in. He never did figure out how in hell he could have hit it.

"After that, he kept an axe in the corner, all the time Maria was gone. When somethin' got after chickens or such, he'd go out and chop it to flinders. But he left that gun strictly alone. Said he was scared the slug would go around in a circle and into the house and kill one of his babies."

Benny looked bewildered. "Howinell did he manage it?" he asked. "A gun is a gun. If it's accurate, anybody ought to be able to hit what he aims at, if he does it right."

"Anyplace else but Cotton County, that may be true," said Solomon Peat. He paused to hand out change for strawberry pop to a procession of youngsters who had finally tired of shooting the B-B gun.

"But here we seem to have two sorts of people. There's the

49

sharpshooters, like everyplace else has, and then there's the world's onliest dullshooter. Old as he is, by now, José still don't touch a firearm of any kind or description. And a good thing, too." Sol spat.

"Life's dangerous enough as it is, with newclear bombs and such. Nobody needs José rampagin' around with a gun in his hand, to boot. That would be just a mite too much."

Benny rose and took up his brown bag of nails. He shook his head and started off down the road.

Will Henry came out of the store with his strawberry pop and sat on the vacated edge of the porch. "You know, Uncle Sol, I'm gettin' to be a real sharpshooter," he said.

Solomon Peat smiled. "And a good thing, too. There's a lot worse things you might be."

X.

FORAY INTO SUNDOWN

"You can't come, and that's that!" said Will Henry. He glared down at Les and Fane. He turned to Tim. "You tell 'em, Tim. You're their big brother...maybe they'll listen to you."

The boy's brown eyes widened. "They will? I didn't never know that, Will Henry. Might as well let 'em come with us. If we don't, they'll go right straight and tell Ma, and then we'll all be in the soup."

Will Henry sighed gustily. He'd never heard of taking little kids along on serious business like this, but it looked necessary. Reconnaissance of the swamp and the river, with an eye to finding a natural spot for baiting Grampa Catfish, seemed to be business for bigger people than Les and Fane.

"You got to remember something," he said, frowning sternly at the younger boys. "No matter what happens—even if you get hurt; even if you get killed, you can't go crying to your folks. You got to act grown up. Understand that?"

The pair nodded, their eyes round in their dark, snub-nosed faces. "Cross our hearts," said Fane, and Les bobbed his head in agreement.

Unfortunately for the proposed expedition, Will Henry's father caught him as he left the house on Saturday morning and assigned him to the lawnmower. It was after two o'clock when he was through and free to go about his own affairs. Grumbling, he made off for Mrs. Bragg's.

He found his troops sitting, wide-eyed, at Solomon Peat's feet, sipping strawberry soda pop and reveling in a particularly hair-raising tale of the Old Graveyard on the hill beyond Possum Creek. Will Henry felt cheated. Not only had they left their project perilously late in the day, but he had almost missed one of Uncle Sol's stories.

"And old Jed, he come slippin' up there, quiet as the grave...." Sol chuckled wickedly. "To dig up Miz Edenly and get that di'mond ring offen her finger. Not a soul was about. Nobody in his right senses goes to a graveyard in the middle of the night, anyway, and he felt morally certain he was goin' to get away with it clean as a whistle.

"The screech owls was quaverin' in the woods fit to make his skin crawl right off his bones, but he kept on, stumblin' over grave markers and barking his shins on footstones, till he come right up to the Edenly tomb.

"It was one of them fancy ones that sticks up out of the ground a ways, with a little fancy roof over the top. He was tickled to death...that meant he wouldn't have to dig to get to the coffin. He heaved a good one to get the top to moving, and once that happened he didn't pause till he had it slipped clean over to one side, just short of falling all the way onto the ground."

Will Henry had now joined the others, round-eyed and entranced. He waited while Sol spat and wiped his mouth, and he could feel chills going up and down his back.

"It made considerable noise, as you might suspect, so he stopped right there for a little and listened for anything amiss. He waited till the owl took up where he left off and the crickets started in again with their ratcheting. He got the lid off the coffin as quiet as rain on grass. There wasn't any smell to speak of, though he'd expected it to be pretty powerful by then, and he was relieved about that, too.

"He reached in to take the dead woman's hand. He'd climbed up on top of the tomb, of course, to reach, and he was leaned way down, with one toe hooked around the tree next to the grave, just to make sure he didn't fall in." Sol grinned suddenly.

"And a good thing, too, 'cause when he pulled on that ring, the dead woman's hand moved, and all of a sudden she had him by the wrist. It was a sure-enough death-grip, that was, pulling hard on him. He come as near as scat fallin' down into the grave with her."

Will Henry felt his heart thud, and beside him Chuck was shivering, despite the heat. "And did he?" he whispered.

"No. Not quite. He held hard with his toe and got his other toe hung over the angle of the tomb, and there he was, held by the wrist by a dead woman. Couldn't get loose, and couldn't turn loose and couldn't think what to do at all.

"It was somewhere around two o'clock when he got there and maybe two-thirty when he found himself in that fix. He knowed there was a lot of the night left, before old Curtis, who mowed the grass and kept up the graves, made it to work the next morning.

"I've heard Jed say, many's the time, that it was the longest night God ever run through his mill. Seemed as if that woman just pulled steady, harder and harder. She'd been a great big woman, weighed around three hundred pounds, and he kept wonderin' what would happen if she really put her back into it. But she didn't, and he hung on till the sun come up.

"Curtis found him, along about eight o'clock. Took him a while to understand what was going on. Then he didn't quite know what to do about it, being as he wasn't supposed to interfere, no way, no how, with the people inside the graves. He run off and got the preacher, and the preacher got hold of the doctor, and by nine-thirty Jed had some real help.

"Turned out Mrs. Edenly wasn't dead at all. Not entirely. In them days, folks wasn't embalmed, like they are now, and she'd been in a sort of coma with just enough life left in her to know somebody was after that ring that she prized more than anything else in the world. Time the doctor looked at her, she was gone, sure enough. They had to break her fingers to get them off from around Jed's wrist."

"But how come she kept pulling?" asked Will Henry.

"Oh, that was Jed doing the pulling, without really realizin' what he was doing. I expect we'd all have done that, in his fix." Sol sighed. "And now that I'm a lot older than I was when I heard that tale, I kind of sympathize with Miz Edenly. Seems like the least folks can do is to let dead folks rest easy in their graves."

Will Henry stood up and indicated to his crew that it was time to go. "Sure was a good story, Uncle Sol," he said. "Even if I did miss the beginning."

"Where you boys going?" asked the patriarch. "It's near too hot for fishing."

"Oh, we thought we'd go down in the woods this side of Sundown," Will Henry said, his tone carefully casual. "Just mess around in the shade, catch a few tadpoles out of one of the creeks, maybe. It's a sight cooler down there than it is here."

"You could go inside and enjoy the air conditioning," suggested Sol, but he didn't sound serious. He hated being shut up inside as much as the boys did.

"Well, you take care not to go into the swamp. I know your folks don't want you in there, and when it's this hot, those old water moccasins are just as bad tempered as they can be. Say, you want a jar for them tadpoles?"

Will Henry felt it was best to stay with his story, and he nodded. "You got one?"

"Right under there. Brought some soap powder down for old Uncle Ned Turner. It'll be nice not to have to carry the jar back home again."

So Will Henry took the quart Mason jar from beneath Sol's chair, slung it by a string to his belt, and led his file of adventurers off toward the swamp.

When the first rank of trees closed behind them, the boys cut away from their former course toward the big woods and angled toward Sundown Swamp. Will Henry felt a qualm, even as he did it. His father would skin him alive, if he found out, but if they were to catch Grampa Catfish they had to get busy. And everyone knew that the big creature roamed the river near the outlet channel from the swamp.

Chuck and Tim were right behind him, and he looked back from time to time to see that Les and Fane were keeping up. Losing the two little boys in the swamp was a guaranteed way to get into big trouble. Again, he headed toward the channel, taking the ridge of solid land and keeping strictly to the main path. When they were well into the heavy growth, however, he saw another smaller path branching away toward the river. He paused.

"We're awful late," he said. "You think that path might go straighter to the river and cut off a lot of distance?"

Tim looked at the track. He turned slowly, observing the trees and the bushes around them. "My uncle uses that, when he hitches up his boat over on Roan's Slough," he said. "Goes right on through, I think he said."

Will Henry stepped off the firm ridge onto the path. Ferns swayed around his ankles, and he looked sharp to see he didn't step on a water moccasin. The ground was softer here, padded with years and years of mulch and silt that had been deposited when the floods came. A flame of cardinal flower showed ahead, and at that spot the path diverged, becoming three separate tracks.

They had come quite a way. He had no intention of going back...the sun was already down in the sky, slanting through chinks in the leaf cover.

He said, "Eeny-meeny-minie-mo," and headed down the middle trail.

Behind him, his troop was unusually quiet. They knew as well as he did that they weren't supposed to be in the swamp at all. They also understood that they knew nothing about their present route.

Their silence was an indictment of their leader, but Will Henry ignored it.

The ground grew wetter and wetter, and the path began to squish gently beneath his sneakers' soles. The trees were bigger, now, and it was darkish beneath their thick-leaved crowns. He had lifted his foot for a step over a log, when something came crashing toward him through the brush ahead. He jumped. He couldn't help it.

Then he heard a bloodcurdling cry from behind. "It's all right— just a deer," he said, as a dim shape whisked out of sight in the trees.

"It ain't all right!" That was Tim, and something was drastically wrong with his voice.

Will Henry, his heart thumping in his throat, moved back along the trail. "Where's Les?" he asked. "Where's Fane?"

"Down there," said Tim, pointing.

He looked, but only the heads of ferns met his gaze. "Where?"

Chuck went onto his knees and tugged up a clump of ferns, revealing a black opening. "They fell in there!"

Tim's face had turned as pale as his natural complexion could manage. "Les? Fane? You all right?" he quavered.

"We in the dark!" came a small voice from beneath their feet. "And they's snakes down here!"

The three older boys looked at each other in horror. They had been warned all their lives not to get into dark, wet places. Moccasins just naturally loved such locations. And now the two little ones were right down there in the worst place any of them could imagine.

Will Henry began pulling up all the ferns rimming the hole. The other two joined in, and when they paused for breath they had uncovered an opening some three feet across. Now that light could get into the hole, they could see that the near side slanted a bit, while the other was undercut. Two small faces stared up at them, their eyes rimmed with white.

Les and Fane had fallen onto a heap of debris and were sitting up against each other, still as death. Around them in an arc squirmed what seemed to be hundreds of cotton-mouth moccasins, some of them coiled, mouths open to reveal the white interiors that looked almost like some kind of vicious flower, others sliding slowly into knots and bulges and loops.

"Help me, Jesus!" said Tim, sliding down to sit flat on the ground.

"We'll get them out!" Will Henry assured him. "I just don't quite know how, yet."

XI.

Moccasin Hole

Will Henry had always done a lot of thinking, but never in all his life had his brain run at such high speed as it did now. First he thought of getting help—that seemed natural, under the circumstances. But then he realized that any adult brought into this situation would blow the whistle on him and his cronies.

"If we get somebody in to help us," he mused aloud, "we'll never again get the chance to catch that catfish. We got to get those boys out by ourselves." He cocked an eye at the bits of sky visible above the treetops. "And we got to do it quick. It'll be dark in another three hours. If we're not all at home by then, there's the devil to pay for us all."

Tim whistled dolefully. "How you goin' to do it? There's more moccasins down there than I ever seen in all my life before. Sure as we stir 'em up the least little bit, they're goin' to bite my little brothers."

"We just have to think. Use our heads! There's got to be a way." Will Henry hunkered down on his heels and stared into the hole. Four pale-rimmed eyes stared back from small faces whose natural brown had gone to a strange shade of ashy gray.

He had to admit, however, that Les and Fane were living up to their promise. They weren't making a sound. He tried to smile down at them, but he was afraid he wasn't making a very good job of it.

The snakes, once they got settled down a bit, seemed to grow calmer. Those that had been coiled were eased up, their heads resting on their top layers of coils, their mouths just about closed. The others continued their eternal squirming and knotting and unknotting around and about each other. Will Henry had heard of moccasin holes, but he had never thought—or wanted—to see one.

He sat back on the damp soil, settling onto the Mason jar Sol had given him. The string he'd tied it with was a long stout one that Mrs. Bragg had taken off a package she got at the store. He stared at the jar. The string. The hole. He bent over to gaze down at the moccasins.

"I wonder...," he began. The others picked up their ears.

"What if we kind of get their attention? There's a spot down here on this side that's pretty far away from where the boys are, and the lip of the hole lies right above the biggest bunch of snakes. And if we got all of 'em over this way, interested in somethin'...hmmm...yep, I think it just might work." He rose to his feet and stared of into the maze of pools and hummocks and trees and brush about them.

"Joe Lacey cut his winter wood down here last fall," he mused. "Didn't he tell you it was right around here?"

Tim thought a moment. Then he nodded. "He said it was right past the biggest old double gum tree he ever seen in his life. Like that one yonder. He got a coon run up it one evening and burnt out the holler up its middle. That's got to be the one, 'cause you can still see the soot from the fire where it comes out the place between the halves."

"You stay here. Keep the boys calm," said Will Henry. "Chuck, you come with me."

It was his general's voice, and that told the others he had everything under control. Just stay calm, that was what it told them.

He tore along a track so faint that only desperation could have allowed him to follow it at all. When he arrived at the blackened sweet gum, he found, as he expected, that Joe Lacey, in his usual slack-twisted way, had left tops and branches strewn all around the spot where he had been cutting. Now the wood was dry, and all the leaves had fallen from the dried branches.

He spotted what he wanted. A top lay at an angle, propped against a hawthorn overgrown with bamboo vine until it looked like an upholstered footstool. Short branches stubbed out from the top, and the stalk was thicker than his leg.

"That ought to be strong enough," he said to Chuck. "Help me break off the ends of the limbs."

They tugged the thing down flat and began breaking off branches, leaving a hand's breadth of wood connected to the trunk. Before they'd done much, Chuck whistled shrilly.

"By golly, Will Henry, I've got to hand it to you. You're makin' a ladder for those boys to climb up on."

Will Henry nodded, his hands busy. "Hurry up," he said. "We've got to get back quick."

It wasn't easy getting the awkward thing through the brush along the path, but with Will Henry on the front end and Chuck handling the heavier butt, they managed. When they got back to the hole, Tim was shivering with tension.

He stared from Will Henry's face to the impromptu ladder and back again. "You want 'em to climb up that? And what about the snakes? They goin' to pull back and be gennelmen and let 'em go without bitin' 'em?" he asked.

"That's what the jar is for," panted Will Henry. "Here, you go and fill it up with water out of that pool over there. Then I'll show you what to do."

While Tim was gone, Chuck and Will Henry positioned the jagged branch. When he came back, carrying the jar carefully to avoid spilling the water, Will Henry took the string and made a sort of yoke around the neck of the jar, with two loops, one on either side, to make it hang steady. Through the loops he put one end of the string and knotted it, pulling the tops of the loops tightly together.

"Now you go over there on that side and let the jar down, real slow. Make it swing and jiggle all you can without spilling everything. You get those snakes all worked up and interested and suspicious. Chuck and me'll tend to the rest."

Tim began letting the jar down into the hole. There was a span of perhaps four feet, just beneath the lip where he lay, and most of the moccasins were in the shady hollow under the bank. They didn't notice the jar at first. He had to toss bits of bark and clods of dirt onto them to make them perk up enough to see what was going on.

They began to wiggle around, then, those below raising their cottony maws and those nearer the hummock where the boys were sitting moving around so they could see what was happening. The closer to the floor the jar got, the more excited the snakes became. When the glass was eighteen inches above the floor of the hole, Chuck and Will Henry began letting the stubby ladder down onto the hummock from the other, slanted side of the hole.

Inch by inch, they moved the thing, pausing when the snakes seemed about to turn their attention toward them, beginning again when they returned to gazing at the intruding jar. When the butt tumped solidly into the hummock, Will Henry felt as if all his strength had run out of him like water from a sink.

Tim, seeing that things were ready to move, joggled the jar hard, making splashes of water dollop over onto the moccasins. The hole filled with angry hisses, and sudden "tinks" told the boys that the reptiles were striking at the glass. Now the whole batch had their attention focused on the jar, forgetting entirely about the earlier intruders.

"Now!" whispered Will Henry.

Les and Fane looked at each other. They stared at their brother and at the glinting, sloshing jar. Then, as quickly as squirrels or mice, they were up the treetop, scampering out of the hole as if propelled by magic.

Tim pulled in the jar and emptied the water carefully onto a mullein stalk beside the path. He wound the string around its neck and tucked the thing under his arm.

Will Henry grinned. "Souvenir?" he asked.

"Naw," said Tim. "My Ma, she uses Mason jars all the time. Don't want to waste this 'un."

But he was grinning, too, his black eyes shining. Once again, Will Henry had proven his mettle. Not one of his companions would ever forget this day.

XII.

The Inflated Flea

Solomon was dozing, propped back in his chair against the wall of the store. Mrs. Bragg swept around the two legs that sat on the faded boards, raising a cloud of dust, and looked as if she would like to jerk the other two out from under him. But she knew all too well that Sol attracted far more customers to her store than her merchandise ever could.

As she thumped back into the building, he opened one blue eye and winked at Will Henry, who was coming out of the store with a bottle of strawberry pop. He perched on the edge of the porch and stared up at Sol appraisingly.

"It's awful hot," he said. "Too hot to fish. Too hot to hunt jaybirds with the popgun. Too hot to walk down and see what Chuck and Tim are doin'." He sighed dolefully, for there is nothing on God's green earth as bored as a small boy on a hot summer's day.

Sol plunked the chair legs down solidly and stared off over the tops of the pine trees. "Reminds me of when I was a boy," he said. "We had some goshawful hot summers, back then, too. No air conditioning helped us cool off, either. Seemed as if the summer used to drag on and on forever. Got so we even missed goin' to school, though you may not credit that. We'd have tried most anything to liven things up." He cocked a bushy white eyebrow at the boy.

"Did I ever tell you about my pet flea?"

Will Henry choked on his pop. "Uncle Sol, you know nobody ever made a pet out of a flea," he gasped.

"Nobody but me, maybe. Why I had that flea so trained up that I could just point to a dog, and he'd hop right onto him. He'd ride around and around till I whistled for him, and then he'd come back and get in the matchbox where I kept him."

Chuck and Tim, followed by Les and Fane, came plodding up

the road, kicking up puffs of straw-colored dust beneath their leathery soles. Even the broiling hot sand of the road didn't penetrate feet that had gone bare since May.

"Here, you go and get yourselves some pop," said Sol. "And get another one for Will Henry...he's just about through with his." He shelled out a handful of quarters and leaned back against the wall again.

When the five were in place along the edge of the porch, leaning against the posts or Mrs. Bragg's huge pots of fern and petunias, he looked off across the treetops again. All of them knew that meant that a story was on its way.

"That flea came near to being the best pet I ever had. But of course I had to go and get fancy. My brother always told me I messed up everything I touched, just by trying to get too cute. In that case, he was dead right. I decided, being as that flea was so smart and so accommodating, I just had to try ridin' him."

Les's eyes went even rounder than usual, as he stared up at the rotund old fellow. "Nobody could ride a FLEA," he protested, around a gulp of pop.

"Well, not in its natural state, I admit," said Solomon. "But I had a lot under my hat besides hair and sweat, believe you me. I had a plan."

Will Henry began to smile. Just a crinkle at each corner of his mouth showed Uncle Sol he knew that one of his spectacular Tall Tales was on its way. Sol didn't let on he noticed, however, as he spat into his snuff can and snapped the lid back on.

"My brother—you recall my tellin' you about Yale?—had an old bicycle that he rode all over creation. He taken odd jobs here and yonder, and that bike got him there and back, though most times he had to stop to patch a tire or fix a spoke or two on the way. Anyway, he had a little old tire pump that he carried along with him.

"I figured it out smooth and smart. Then I borrowed Yale's pump and got a hollow needle from the football coach at school. You know, the sort they used to pump up footballs with? And I screwed that sucker right onto the pump. Then I stuck the other end in Ezra's mouth."

"Who's Ezra?" asked Will Henry.

"Why, my flea, of course. He just sort of looked like an Ezra to me. Anyway, he chomped down on it, and I began to pump, real fast, before he could turn loose.

"You never saw nothing like it. Why that flea began to swell and swell, and the more I pumped the bigger he got, like one of these here little tiny balloons that you can blow up to be bigger than a watermelon.

"Got so he was the size of Ma's footstool. I figured I better stop there. Didn't want to blow the poor thing clean to flinders, you know."

Will Henry was shaking now, and Chuck had buried his face on Tim's back and was laughing out loud.

Sol ignored them. He sighed deeply before continuing, "I rode that critter all over Pa's farm. When the wind'd blow real good and hard, we could sail right up over the woods. I thought about that, when I used to see Slewfoot Sally flyin' on her mule, I tell you. There's just nothing like it in this world."

"The world's first floating flea," gasped Will Henry.

"Prob'ly. Likely, in fact. I let my little brother William take a ride, now and again, though Ma didn't rightly approve of it. She thought it was Cruelty to Animals or some such. Yale wouldn't even take notice. He thought it was just little-boy foolishness, which I guess in a way it was."

Mrs. Bragg came out on the porch and stared around to see if the boys were messing up her porch. But they just kept drinking their red bottles-full, being customers instead of pests, and she went inside again.

"That turned into a plumb good summer, let me tell you. William and me tried a time or two to ride double, but that was askin' a mite much, even of Ezra. So we taken turns, and Yale was good about lending us his pump every morning before he rode off to work. Got so Ezra looked a little flabby, when we let him down in the evening, but I was too young and ignorant to notice that much.

"Anyway, it got on toward fall, and we began to get itchy about goin' back to school. The west wind come up, like it sometimes does that time of year, all gusty and fitful, and we'd get on Ezra and ride him till it felt like some kind of a roller coaster.

"There'd been a fellow over in the next county got him a airplane. We was all excited about that, and he come to the Cotton County Fair and did stunts that would raise your hair and curl it and turn it white, all in one operation.

"Naturally, Will and me wanted to try the same thing when we got back home. I taken Ezra up when the wind was just awful. It felt like riding a balloon, and the downdrafts would catch us, then an updraft would come along and take us away up, and then another downdraft would shoot us down again. If Ezra hadn't of been a world champion jumper, we'd have been in trouble a lot of times."

Sol began to look a bit sad. "And as you might guess, I got too cute. Again. I'd been making Ez do barrel rolls, when there come a great big gust. It sailed us right onto the top of Mama's summer house in the flower beds. Bein' as he was in the middle of a roll, Ez didn't have his feet down, and he rolled over me and right off the edge, into Mama's Paul Scarlet Climber rose vine."

There came a muffled gasp from Les.

"Yep. You guessed it. It popped him, just like those big balloons you get at the county fair. There come a crack like a firecracker, and then there was nothing left of him but bits of flea skin, and it shrunk right back up till you couldn't even see the pieces. I fell into the vines, too, and it taken William and me both to get me out." Sol took out his blue bandana and wiped his eyes. Then he refolded the cloth carefully and returned it to the pocket of his overalls.

"And that was the end of Ezra and the summer, both to once. Never again in all my life have I had anything like either of 'em. And William's heart was nigh broke, too. He was too young to know that not every flea in the world was an Ezra, so he kept tryin' to pump up little old wild fleas. Got 'em in his hair and his clothes till Mama put her foot down.

"'No more fleas, no way,' she told him, and that was that. But I still think of old Ezra, every now and then when it's real hot and the summer is half gone, and the wind begins to get gusty. But I guess that sort of thing is for when you're young. I'm too old for such foolishness, now."

Les stared at Tim. Tim shook his head, and Sol nodded in agreement. "Don't go tryin' that, boys. There just ain't any more fleas the caliber of Ezra, I swear to you. And I sure as heck don't want all your Mamas coming after me for getting her kids full of fleas while they try out the method."

Mrs. Bragg came out onto the porch. "Will Henry, your Ma phoned. Said for you to come home and mow the yard, right now. She said you got in too much of a hurry, the other day, and left a whole strip on the other side of the hedge. You scat now, you hear me?"

Will Henry drained the second bottle of pop and put the empty into the case waiting for the cold drink man. "Yes'm, Mrs. Bragg. I'll do that."

He turned and winked at Sol. Sol grinned broadly and winked back, his eyes still full of devilment that old Ezra would probably have recognized right off.

XIII.

Midsummer Doldrums

Will Henry couldn't quite figure it out. Somehow, his folks seemed to sense that he had a project in hand...one that they wouldn't approve of. They kept him so busy around the house and yard that he couldn't find the time to get his crew together and do any more poking around in the swamp until the steamy-hot days of late July made it too uncomfortable, anyhow.

When that happened, his Dad seemed to know it, too. Things let up, and he found himself with too much time on his hands and nothing to do with it. That, of course, meant a trip to Mrs. Bragg's store. Maybe Uncle Sol could come up with a tale that would keep small boys from going loco in the heat.

He got there early on a Thursday morning, before the sun was entirely up above the pine trees. The air smelled wonderful. Still cooled with dew, it hinted at sun-warmed pine straw and rosin-weed and there was a hint of the fermented smell of the river, moving sluggishly amid rampant water weeds, and of the swamp.

He knew he was too early...Uncle Sol tended to his chickens and milked his cow before he walked up to the store. But Will Henry sat on the porch, waiting for Mrs. Bragg to come in her Chevy and open up. People often stopped on their way to work to pick up lunch materials, and she opened by seven-thirty to catch that bit of her trade.

He fumbled in his pocket to make sure he had the price of a strawberry pop. As long as he was a customer, he was welcome to sit on the porch. If he turned into just another small boy, he would be sent off with a bug in his ear.

Sure enough, she pulled up in a trickle of dust and parked the Chevy under one of the chinaberry trees. Once she saw him, she almost frowned, but he jingled his change in his pocket, and the lines smoothed away.

The pop was heavenly cold, having been in the machine all night without anyone disturbing it and letting in the warmer air. Will Henry took it onto the porch in time to see Sol trudging up the road. He paused from time to time to wipe his forehead with his blue bandana, for it was already getting hot, and the sun was now scorching the dust, as the tree-shadow retreated beneath the wall of pines.

"Hi, Uncle Sol!" Will Henry shouted. He hopped off the porch and flew along the road, white puffs of dust flying up beneath his horny feet. He made a flying circle around the old man before adopting a more sober gait.

He fell into step beside his great-uncle. "I'm bored out of my gourd," he said. "There's just not a thing happening, and nothing is going to happen, and I'm ready to bust wide open."

"It's that time of the year," Sol agreed. He looked at the porch steps as if they meant a climb of Himalayan proportions. Then he sighed deeply and heaved his bulk up them.

"Mrs. Bragg? You got the coffee pot on?" he called.

"Ready in a minute," came her gruff reply, and he sighed and settled into his chair.

"You know, you ought to be enjoying this. It won't be long before you've got to go back to school. Then you'll think about all this time you had on your hands, and you'll wish you'd done something with it."

"I know," sighed the boy. "But darned if I can think of anything worth doing. It's just too hot to go fishin' or walk in the woods or hunt jaybirds with my B-B gun."

"Makes me think of when I was a boy," said Sol. "I had the same old problem. Seems to be just built into kids and summertime. But when I went back to school—hoo-boy! I could think of a million things I should of done. Course, it was a lot different, when I went to school. By damn, that was near seventy years ago! Seems strange...." He seemed to go off into a reverie, but Will Henry jogged him back to the present.

"How different?" He looked as skeptical as he could manage. "School's school, and how can it get very different, no matter when it was?"

"You'd be amazed," said Sol.

Mrs. Bragg came out of the store with Sol's big mug, on which some wit had written LIAR'S AWARD in Magic Marker. "Here, Sol. Wake you up."

As she stomped back into the store, Sol took a sip and closed his eyes. "That woman's got a lot of faults, but makin' bad coffee's not one of 'em," he said.

He puffed his cheeks out two or three times, got his bulk comfortable in his chair, and looked back down at Will Henry, who was making his pop last as long as possible. "You want to know about my school days? It's a good morning for that.

"First off, there wasn't no school bus, in them days. We walked, William and Yale and me, two and a half miles to get there. When it was wet, we weighed ten pounds more apiece when we got there than we did when we set out. Each foot picked up mud and picked up mud, till we could hardly walk. Wasn't so bad when we could go barefoot, but Ma wouldn't hear of that when it was cold. Too many folks died of noomony in them days."

He grunted, a chuckle bubbling up from deep in his belly. "I recall one cold morning. We'd loaded up our lunches in syrup buckets. Ma baked biscuit every morning, and she'd put each of us a half dozen, hot from the oven. She'd poke a hole in each with her finger and pour in melted butter and cane syrup. By the time it got to lunchtime, we'd be ready to put in more syrup, and she'd fill a snuff bottle with the stuff and send it along, one bottle to one bucket." He began laughing aloud.

"We had to cut through the pasture and Mr. Jamison's place to get to the road, and that took us across Bobcat Creek. On this partic'lar morning, the creek was froze solid. I mean it was cold! And Jamison's cows had come down to get a drink and couldn't and was standing around bellowin' their heads off.

"Yale was the biggest of us by far, and he run out on the ice and slipped and busted his butt. We laughed, and the cows milled around and one of 'em got onto the ice and began the dadgummedest shenanigans you ever saw in your life.

"William scooted over and drove some stragglers out on the ice, and I got the idea and did my share. Yale brought in the rest. We hooted and hollered and run them pore cows along on that ice, and they was plenty upset.

"They skated this way and that, and they fell to the front and skidded to the back and piled up in heaps, and you never heard such a godawful bawling and moaning in history. Sounded like the Last Trump, and of course Jamison heard 'em, finally.

"He come scallyhooting through the woods, mad as a hornet, with his shotgun loaded and ready. We heard him before he got there, and we'd already gone up on the other side of the creek and was hot-footin' it toward the road when he shot over our heads into the treetops.

"I mean, dead twigs and chunks of ice and old leaves come raining down on us. We took off and ran like rabbits, I mean to tell you. And he kept shootin' and yellin', and we ran faster and faster, just knowing he was going to take it into his head to blow us to flinders."

Now Sol was laughing, wiping his eyes with his bandana, his shoulders heaving. "Well, long about the time we hit the road, that syrup, which had been gettin' nice and warm in there with the hot biscuits, got mightily joggled up. The snuff bottles begun blowing their corks, and the corks'd hit the tin lids of the syrup buckets, and every time it happened, we knowed we was shot. It was three scared kids got to school that morning, you'd better believe."

Will Henry was giggling. "That was a lot better than riding any old school bus," he said. "Everything is so...so cut and dried, nowadays."

"I 'spect so," said Sol. "Take for instance Jack Cody's goat-cart. Jack was crippled. Nowadays they'd prob'ly call what he got polio, but back then he just got sick and when he got well his legs was all shriveled up and he couldn't walk. His folks fixed him up a little cart with a big old billy goat to pull it. He hitched the whole thing up himself, too. They made him a rolling chair, so he could get around.

"He'd get to school and drive right under the schoolhouse—it was built way up on stilts so when the river got up it wouldn't flood. He'd unhitch the goat and tie him to one of the pillars, with a chunk of hay out of the cart to keep him satisfied.

"There was nothing we liked, we big boys, better than pretendin' we had to go out to the privy behind the school and cutting back under there to untie Jack's goat. That meant the whole school got turned out to chase that animal through the woods. We got out of many a half day of school, that way."

Will Henry had chirked up remarkably. "How did Jack get up the steps into the schoolhouse?" he asked.

"Oh, when he was all done with haying his goat and tying him up, he'd call, and Mr. Roberts, our teacher, would go down and carry him up. Somebody else would take the chair up, so he could get around the schoolroom. We was kin, most of us, and that little old school was a little like a family. More than they are now, by a long shot."

Will Henry drained his pop bottle. "I'd have liked it better then," he said. "There's no goat carts and no woods and no icy creeks anywhere in miles of our school. Just asphalt and cars and brick walls and mean teachers."

"Oh," said Sol, "Mr. Roberts could be pretty stern." He drank the last of his coffee and set the mug on the floor at his feet.

"He used to begin every school day with an exercise aimed right at me."

"What was that?" Will Henry had already risen to go.

"Why, the first thing he did, every morning of the world, was to get out his paddle and whale the daylights out of me and stand me in the corner. He said he knowed he'd have to do it sooner or later, so he just got it out of his way so he could get down to his teachin'."

Will Henry cocked his head and looked at Uncle Sol. Something in those bright eyes told him that the boy he'd been hadn't been quelled. Not even by years of school and whalings.

He hopped off the porch and started toward Tim's house. After a few steps, he turned back. "Did he ever quit doing that?" he asked.

Sol grinned. "Nope. Eight years I went to school to him, and eight years he whaled me good every morning. I 'spect, if he was still alive, he'd be doin' that to this day."

Mrs. Bragg's mordant tones floated out of the store. "As well he should," she said.

Will Henry laughed all the way to Les's.

XIV.

A NASTY SORT OF THING

It was raining; the sort of drizzly weather that sometimes socks in for a day at a time in July was soaking the pine woods, cooling off the day considerably (though temporarily), and keeping the porch of Mrs. Bragg's store occupied with people who dreaded stepping off into the rich red mud of the road.

Sol, his chair hitched back against the wall, had just finished loading up a fresh chew of snuff and was shooting the breeze with Lazarus Evans, who'd been a deputy in his day. To hear him talk, he'd been a cross between the Lone Ranger and Superman.

Will Henry, however, had heard his Dad talking about Laz, and he knew the old codger had been luckier than most and more cautious than many. Even so, the talk of long-dead desperadoes was lively stuff on a dull day. He hitched himself closer and listened hard.

"Deader'n a doorknob," Laz was saying. "Tell me I couldn't shoot in them days! I was a crack shot, and no fooling."

Uncle Sol cocked his bright blue eyes and frowned. "Didn't I hear somethin' about it being Sheriff Tomlin that done that bit of shootin'?" he asked, his tone innocent as a dove.

Laz's weathered face went a darker shade of red. "There's folks that put that around, but I was there, Solomon Peat! I pulled that trigger, and I shot that booger dead. Didn't touch a hair of the kid he was holding in front of him, either."

Sol sighed. He knew he'd never make Laz admit that he couldn't hit the side of a barn on a bright day with no crosswind, Will Henry understood. He'd heard the old fellows at it before.

"You recall Doctor Benedict?" Sol asked. "He was old as the hills when we were both sprats, but I can remember him. Big tall fellow, skinny as a rail. His black coat always looked as if he'd forgot to take the hanger out of it before he put it on."

"Now that was a real strange thing," mused Laz. "And he was never found, from that day to this. I've wondered and wondered about that case. The sheriff used to talk about it, back when I was a deputy. It upset folks for miles around, and some still remember it and wonder, too."

"As well they should," said Sol. "He was the onliest doctor in fifty miles, after old Doc Ballard died. After he was gone, you had to go all the way to Tyler or Shreveport to get real doctorin'. And back then, that wasn't near as easy to do as it is now."

"There's been many a tale told about that, all of 'em guesses," said Laz. "And nobody never will know for certain."

"Well I know," said Sol, his tone solemn. "My Pa told me. He never told another living soul as long as he lived, for he was scared to mention it, even way out in the middle of the field where he told me, with nobody there but the mules and the corn."

"Wait a minute," said Will Henry, his tone respectful but firm. "I don't know about Doctor Benedict. If you're going to solve a big mystery, first tell me what it was."

Sol grinned. "Rafe Benedict come to East Texas from London, England," he said. "My Pa told me he'd gone to school in Scotland and was a real fine surgeon, as well as the other sort of doctor. Mostly, of course, he delivered babies and tended gunshot wounds and broke legs, but he was good at everything he done, and he didn't lose many patients. The ones he lost were mostly old and wore out, anyway."

"So what happened to him? What made the mystery?" asked the boy.

"One night in November there come a knock on his door. His housekeeper—his wife was dead, by then—answered it and there stood Leander Smith, dripping wet and half froze. Wanted the doctor, he said, to come see after his brother.

"Now everybody knowed that the Smith boys fought like two tomcats under a tin tub. Besides that, they was mean as sore-eared bears, even when they was well and happy. Doc Benedict was tired...he'd delivered twins that day, and it'd been a long, hard business. So Miz Hester hated to go and wake him up and send him out into that nasty weather, particularly as she didn't care a hang if one or both of the Smith brothers died or not.

"Still, he'd give her strict orders. She wasn't ever to turn a soul away, no matter who or when. So she went and woke him and he got up and set out in his buggy, with his old black mare Nellie. Leander didn't say another word to Miz Hester, just climbed in with the doctor and they taken off.

"And that was the very last that any living soul, except for Leander Smith, ever saw of Doctor Raphael Benedict."

"But what about his horse and buggy? Surely when they found those, they knew pretty well where he'd been," said Will Henry.

"They never found them, neither. Not a trace of black Nellie or that buggy ever come to light. There was talk the buggy might have gone into the bottomless pond over to Mill's Slough, but that was away to hell and gone out of the way to the Smiths' house. A black mare would be easy to sell, if you taken her a long ways off, but nobody ever set eyes on Nellie again. Not to know her."

"But what about Leander Smith? What did he say?"

"Oh, Leander claimed the doc come and saw his brother, all right, and then took off again for home. Said he never knowed he didn't get there till the sheriff come asking about him. And nobody could prove any different, though the brother had died and Leander had buried him on the family land beside their Ma and Pa before anybody ever knowed he was dead."

Will Henry sighed. It was just the sort of mystery he loved best.

Laz nodded. "And there it's stood ever since, sixty years if it's a day."

Sol grunted. "Pa was out that night, too. And he was in the north part of the county, not too far from the Smiths'. His sister's husband had died the day before, and Pa went over to sit up with the body that night. Got off late, because of a sick cow, on his old horse Mose. Mose hated to leave the barn on a night like that, and he poked along and shied at everything in sight, and he ended up by throwin' Pa right off into the mud and takin' off for home.

"Pa was tired and wet and cold and mad, and he was just about to head home, too, when he thought that he was a sight nearer his sister's house. At least, he could dry out and get warm and maybe borrow some of the dead man's clothes, even if it did mean sitting up all night with the corpse. So he trudged along through the mud to a grassy field, and he crossed into that so's his feet wouldn't get so heavy with pickin' up that wet yellow clay mud they have up there.

"When a buggy come tearin' along from the direction of Smiths', he saw it. It had a lantern dangling from the stanchion, and he was off in the field in the dark, so the driver couldn't see him at all. He started to run to catch up with it and get a ride, but about the time he was close enough to recognize Nellie and the doc's buggy, the mare turned off onto the track leading down to the Nichayac River." Sol wiped his brow with his bandana and took a swig of his neglected Coke.

"Well, Pa might be tired and wet and cold, and he might be mad as a six-shooter at his horse, but he still had a bump of curiosity as big as a house. He turned off right after that buggy, running to keep up. It was flyin' along, bumping over roots and rocks and into ruts, but he knowed it wasn't but about a half mile to the river, and he stuck to it.

"When he come up close to the buggy again, the thing had stopped. Before he could get closer, there come a crack like a pistol shot, and the mare dropped in her tracks, right there in the circle of light, still hitched to the rig and lying between the shafts.

"And then he seen Leander Smith come into the light, dragging a long, limp body that just had to be Doctor Benedict. He laid it out alongside the mare, and Pa knowed in his soul they was both dead. He understood, too, that Smith would add him to the tally, if he so much as breathed loud enough for him to hear. Them Smiths was poison, and he had knowed that all his life."

Laz leaned forward, his eyes wide. "It was his bounden duty to go to the sheriff and tell him, once he got clear!" the old man said.

"Just like Ab Duncan did when Smith shot his uncle Dan?" asked Sol. "And Leander went after him and killed him, too, and the sheriff looked the other way, because at that time there was forty-leven danged Smiths in the county, and every one of 'em would have come gunnin' for him if he'd arrested their kin?"

He joggled gently on his hickory splint chair, his expression sad. "No, Pa had a young family and a big farm, and he didn't intend to be planted before his spring crop. He lay down in the mud and weeds and brush and watched, quiet as a lizard.

"Leander got out the doctor's black bag and the keen little knives and the saws and such. He begun to cut the old fellow up into fillets and chunks and bundles. He'd carve a while and saw a while, and Pa said it was tough work cuttin' up the doctor, but it was a sight worse when it come to cutting up that horse."

"So that's what happened to Nellie," mused Laz. "She was so spoiled, she'd have come home, no matter who he sold her to. I figured, somehow, that she was dead. Leander couldn't risk havin' her turn up again."

"Exactly," said Sol. "Then Pa got a notion of what he was going to do. That track ended a quarter of a mile above the old alligator hole in the river. It was November and cold and rainy, but it always warmed up again after a while, and them big old gators would be hungry then. And chunks of doctor and chunks of horse would be right down their alleys.

"He watched that man lug a whole man and a entire horse, bit by bit, out of sight into the dark and then come back empty-handed. It got even darker and nastier, but Leander kept workin'. When he was done with the carcasses, he taken the buggy apart with the axe Doc carried with him and pitched it into the river, piece by piece.

"And that is what happened to Doctor Raphael Benedict of London, England. Pa wanted mighty bad to tell what he'd seen, but every time he thought about it, he recalled Ab Duncan's widow cryin' at the grave, and he pulled back. He decided that Leander Smith might have got in a little over his head, this time, and maybe he'd think hard before he taken on something as hard as the job he'd just done.

"In fact, with his brother gone and nobody to fight with, he did settle down pretty good. At least, he kept strictly to hisself and didn't bother a soul that Pa knowed about."

Will Henry was thinking, his brow furrowed. "But why did Smith kill the doctor in the first place? I just don't understand that."

Sol nodded. "Pa figured maybe Leander had shot or knifed his brother Fee, and that was why he come for the doctor in the first place. Or maybe he beat him to a pulp with a axe handle—they done that sort of thing, from time to time, did the Smiths. And maybe Fee died before they got there and Benedict got one look and made noises about callin' in the law. Leander knowed just what to do about things like that."

Lazarus shook his head. "Who'd of thought I'd ever find out what happened? And why did you keep it so close and quiet all these years? They're all gone, now."

"There was still a lot of them Smiths left for a long time," said Sol, "and I didn't care to get planted premature, either. Anyhow, they buried Hezekiah Smith last week, over to Little Grove church-yard, and he was the last of all that breed of Smiths. I figure with 'em all gone, I can say what I like about Leander, without any fear of consequences." He grinned at Will Henry.

"And if some little offshoot cousin or such comes after me, why I figure I've had a good run for my money, already."

Will Henry frowned at him, wondering what he could do for entertainment, if anything ever happened to Uncle Sol. But about that time the rain let up, and Les and Fane came sloshing up the road barefoot, in cutoffs, and he let it go.

A world without Uncle Sol in it was just unthinkable, and that was that.

XV.

THE POSSUM-CATS

School had started. Solomon Peat always hated that, for it meant that the most absorbed and responsive audience he had would be absent from the porch of Mrs. Bragg's store until after three-thirty. He made do with the straggle of old codgers who played dominoes or occasional salesmen and old ladies who lived alone and hadn't anything to hurry off for, but he lived for the moment when Will Henry and Chuck and Tim and Les and Fane mooched down the road, books in their carry-alls, full of chatter about events on the school bus.

They were always ready for a story, and Sol made it a point to have a particularly good one ready for the end of the first day of school. This third day of September was no exception.

When the boys were settled with their inevitable strawberry pop, he leaned his chair back against the wall and folded his hands over his portly stomach. "Guess you fellows are mighty glad school started," he said, sounding almost serious.

There came a concerted groan from his young listeners. He chuckled. "I recall when I was about your age," he said to Will Henry. "I hated school like poison. But my brothers and I found a lot of things to take our minds off our troubles. I remember one fall when Ma and Pa had to go off to a funeral over to Winston. It took three days, back then, to go and come, the roads being so bad that you just went from one mud hole to the next, getting stuck and cussing and going on to get stuck again."

"Why didn't they pave 'em?" asked Chuck, around the neck of his bottle.

"There wasn't a paved road in this entire part of the country, back then," said Sol. "No cars. Just wagons and buggies and horse-back, that was the way you traveled. And these red clay roads would get so deep in mud that you had to take off into the woods and make your own road, sometimes. Fact is, I've seen the woods for half a mile on either side of a ford just tore up altogether where folks went round till that got terrible, then went further round, and so on.

"So you can see why it took my folks three days to go and come the fifty miles to Winston, and another day to go to Aunt Hassie's funeral. Which left my brothers and me all by our lonesomes in the house." A wicked glint twinkled in his blue eyes.

"Turned out we wasn't a bit bored. What I didn't think of, one of the others would, though Yale was a lot older and thought of a lot of things Will and me didn't even dream of. So we'd come home from school and wrastle the hogs for a while, just to get the steam out of our systems. Then we'd pester Ma's chickens. Always did like to see a old hen get hit in the tail feathers with a chinaberry and go squawking up in the air, then turn around like a old maid schoolteacher that's just been pinched on the rump, looking for the guilty party."

Mrs. Bragg came onto the porch to check whether the boys were being hangers-on, which meant they were empty-handed, or customers, which meant they held bottles of pop. They carefully reserved the last third of their rations, sipping carefully to make it go as far as possible. Satisfied, she clumped back inside and left them to Uncle Sol and his first story of the school year.

"Well, by the time they'd been gone for a couple of days, we'd done all the things we'd been told to make sure we didn't do. We'd tasted the concord grape wine and made ourselves pretty sick doing it, too. We'd chawed some tobacco Yale got from the men he worked with. We'd dirtied all the dishes and sat in the parlor on the best chairs in our work clothes. Just about every kind of devilment we could imagine, we'd done." His slow grin crawled across his wide face.

"And then William found the old calico cat's kittens. There was six of 'em, all colors you ever heard of for cats. They was just right for running and scampering and fighting each other and hissing and spitting like tiny little tigers. We deviled those little critters till old Callie took 'em off under the house to get 'em out of our way. And that left us at loose ends again, till Yale proposed we go hunting with Pa's possum dog."

The boys were leaning forward, their drinks forgotten. If there was anything they loved, it was one of Uncle Sol's hunting stories.

"We loosed old Rock and got the rifles and the shotgun and the lantern, and one night we taken off through the woods. Rock found a scent pretty quick, and he headed for the tall timber. Course a pos-

sum ain't like a coon. He don't run and fight and generally raise
hell. He just goes up into a hollow tree and lies low, but Rock followed his scent and found the tree where that possum was hiding."

Sol waited politely while a couple of the old codgers moved
away from their domino table and moseyed toward home. When
they were gone, he set his hands on his knees and sighed.

"The hollow was about six feet up, and we didn't even have to
set a fire at the bottom to drive the possum out. Yale reached in with
a forked stick and twisted it round and round in that critter's hide till
it was tight as a tick. Then he hauled her out."

"Her?" That was Will Henry.

"Yessir, it was a old she-possum with a whole load of little ones
on her back, holding on with all their might and main. They was just
a tad smaller than those kittens, and we every one of us got the same
idea at the same time."

"What idea?" That was Chuck, who had let his bottle droop until a red dribble stained the sand below the edge of the porch.

"You just wait and see. We took the whole shebang home with
us in a gunny-sack, and time we got there we was tired out. We shut
the possum up in one of Ma's chicken sheds, the little kind where
you put hens that just hatched out a brood, and we knowed the wire
would keep even the little 'uns inside.

"You better believe we went off to school the next day with
heavy feet. We'd have give our eye teeth to stay home, but we
knowed that Ma would forgive us drinking her wine and spitting tobacco in her flowerpots and making sit-marks on the best sofy, but
she'd never in this world leave off whipping on Will and me if we
skipped school. And Yale had to go to work, too, so it wouldn't
have been that much fun without him, anyway."

"But what did you do with 'em, Uncle Sol?" asked Tim. His
black eyes were shining, and his very toes were curled with curiosity.

"That evening when we got back, we ate our supper all nice and
proper. We even taken baths, which would have surprised Ma and
Pa considerable. Then we built up a fire, for a norther had come rip-
ping in that day, and we got those kittens, which Yale had crawled
under the house to catch. We put the possum in a big box in the parlor, and we put the kittens in another box by the fireplace.

"Yale would take a kitten out of their box, and I'd take a possum out of their box, and William would hold the kitten's legs so it
couldn't scratch us to pieces, and we'd pop a possum right onto that
cat's back.

76

"When we turned loose of the first one, that little black sucker took off like a skyrocket. Shot straight up the wall, leaving claw-marks in Ma's wallpaper all the way. I swear to God, boys, that cat ran right across the ceiling, upside down, and down the other wall."

"But how did the possum hang on?" asked Fane. "Seems like it'd fall off, with the cat jumping around that way."

"Son, when the Good Lord made little possums, he meant for 'em to do one thing and just one thing, and that was to hang on come hell or high water. Time we got all six of them kittens fixed up with six of the possums, that parlor looked like some kind of crazy house at the fair.

"Kittens was zooming up and around and over and under and across, and me and Yale and William was standing in the middle of the room yelling and laughing and jumping up and down till we almost cried. I never seen anything like that before or since, and I still can hear them kittens spitting and cussing as they went, trying to get rid of their riders.

"But the more shenanigans they pulled, the harder them possums held on, and finally the cats just naturally run down entire and had to lie down on the floor. They kept twitching and jerking, but for once in history a whole litter of kittens was plumb too exhausted to wiggle. When we taken the possums off, they was still frisky. Looked as if they'd have enjoyed another ride, but we was fresh out of able cats, by that time, and we knowed better than to pester old Callie with such nonsense. She'd have clawed our ears off."

Sol sighed, his eyes bright. "Course, the parlor wasn't never quite the same again. We tried to glue up the holes in Ma's ecru wallpaper with pink roses on it, but she seen the marks the first time she set foot in the room. Not to mention the cat messes we never quite managed to clean up so there wasn't any smell.

"We set real easy for a week or so, and Yale had his wages took till he could pay for another roll of wallpaper to match up with the other. But none of us really felt bad a bit. We'd meet each other on the playground at school, Will and me, and he'd wink and I'd giggle, or vice-versa, and we'd fall out laughing.

"Nossir, there's some things that's worth the price, and seeing those kittens flying around the parlor with the possums holding on for dear life was one of 'em. Young folks nowadays don't seem to think of things like that any more."

"And thank the Lord for that!" came Mrs. Bragg's gruff voice through the wall of the store.

XVI.

KINGDOM COME CEMETERY

Though school had begun and September was rolling right along, it was still hot. The cooler nights dissolved into muggy misery by ten o'clock, and the afternoons were steamy. Will Henry and his chums seldom found the time to visit Mrs. Bragg's, on school days, but Saturdays were different.

After chores were done and parents satisfied that homework was in hand, the boys headed for the store and Uncle Sol like homing pigeons. Sol, after a week-long drought of salesmen too busy to listen and old people who had heard all his tales too many times, was ready for them with newer and better stories, too.

Will Henry, cutting through the woods to save time, found himself lying flat on his stomach, his nose buried in leaf mould. Something had tripped him, and he got up on hands and knees to check it out.

Among the dead leaves of many years, he found something hard and flat, and he brushed away the debris to look at his find. It was a stone, native brown-gray rock, cut into a rough slab. Dirt filled the cracks, but once he dug it out of the lines, he saw words cut into the thing:

ROBERT ABLES
HE WAS ABLE TO SHOOT
BUT HE DIDN'T DODGE
WORTH A DAMN
DIED April 4, 1889
Age about 30

Will Henry sat up, his heart thumping in his throat. He never had heard of anybody being buried right out in the woods like this. If this man had been a stranger, why had someone taken the time and trouble to carve the stone for him? And what had been the cause of his death—besides not dodging fast enough?

The boy rose and scuffed his feet through the debris, looking for more graves. Old cemeteries weren't unusual in the East Texas woods...generations of people had lived and died in the big woods country, after all, and almost a hundred years of that time had been spent in a frontier-like situation, with no organized way of dealing with matters like burying the dead. You tended to your own, and that was that. His own grandparents were buried in Shallowby Cemetery, where the gravediggers were always digging into old graves that had been lost and forgotten for years.

He found another stone, flat among the leaves. It was smaller, about a foot square, with only a short inscription:

ROBBIE
TOO YOUNG TO DIE
Age 6 mos.

Will Henry was almost hopping up and down with excitement. Was Robbie the child of Robert Ables? Maybe Uncle Sol would know. But first he had to be certain there were no more graves here in the woods.

He searched for quite a time, but no more stones were to be found. This was sandy loam, gray-tan in color, and once he knew what to look for, the dark stone showed up distinctly against the soil. When he was sure he had located all that was to be found, he dashed away toward Mrs. Bragg's, leaping over sawvine tangles and whipping through huckleberry bushes.

When he came in sight of the store, pelting, now, down the dusty road, he saw Uncle Sol reared back in his chair, the other boys sitting by his feet. Already they had pop bottles in their hands, and his mouth watered as he pounded up and halted.

"Uncle...Sol! Found a grave...back in the woods! Man

named...Robert Ables!" he panted.

Sol held out a dollar bill. "You go and wet your whistle before you try to talk," he said. "Then come back out here and tell us what you've found. I may just remember the name of Robert Ables."

Will Henry, his face feeling as if it was about to burst, secured the cold strawberry pop and went back out to sit on the porch. Chuck, Tim, Les, and Fane were waiting, swinging their legs off the edge of the porch and watching Miss Zelda Ellinghurst change a tire on her bicycle in the shade of the chinaberry tree. Her skinny elbows were jerking sharply as she put the thing back together and set the bicycle on its wheels.

As Will Henry came out of the store, she came zinging past, her bike purling up a fine strand of dust behind the tires. He waved, and she nodded, her chin almost poking a hole in her collarbone.

He sat beside Chuck and turned to Uncle Sol. "I cut through the woods, and I fell down...tripped over something that turned out to be a tombstone. It was cut deep, and when I dug out the dirt it said something about Robert Ables, who could shoot straight but couldn't dodge. And I looked around and found a baby's grave, too. Robbie, his name was, and he died when he was little bitty."

Solomon stared down at him, his face intent as he searched his memory. "Robert Ables...hmmm. Name rings a bell. Sure does. But I can't quite get a handle on it. Mrs. Bragg!" His voice rose as he called the storekeeper from her rocking chair behind the counter. "You recall a tale about a Robert Ables?"

She came thumping out and dropped into one of the chairs kept for the domino players. "Sol, you've got to be getting old. You mean you don't remember about Kingdom Come?"

Sol's chair legs thudded to the floor, as he sat upright and straightened his glasses. "My Lord! Kingdom Come—and Robert Ables—and Malissa Convers! I haven't thought about that business for...must be forty or fifty years!"

"You would if your own family'd been involved in the mess," the woman replied. "Malissa was my grandmother's aunt. The family's never forgot, and probably never will, though we're not all broke up because others have."

She looked up to see the bread man coming down the road. "About time! Had to call him out of Tompkins, because he whizzed right by and didn't call on me yesterday. He wasn't a bit happy, but right's right, and why should my Saturday customers do without bread because he's too lazy to do his job?" She hurried into the store, followed very soon by the delinquent bread man.

"So what about Robert Ables and the Kingdom Come Cemetery?" asked Will Henry, around a mouthful of strawberry flavored liquid. "And why is he buried in the woods? That's no cemetery around there. There isn't another stone at all."

"No. You're right, that's not a cemetery. Just a spot that was handy at the right time. Now I think about it, it's prob'ly just about the only thing Robert Ables had a thing to do with that turned out to be handy at all. Thing was, he'd riled Pat Germany so bad that even dead, old Pat wouldn't let him be."

"Tell us about it," Tim said, settling himself against one of the porch posts. "Sounds like a corker of a story."

Sol leaned his chair back again and stared off over the pines. His eyes, as they did when he was assembling the parts of a story, seemed to see into some other time and place, which Will Henry felt sure they actually did.

"About—let's see—this is nineteen and seventy-eight. Hmmm. About ninety or ninety-five years ago, now, Malissa Convers was the prettiest gal in Cotton County. But she was feisty, too, and wouldn't take no sass off nobody, male or female. The boys that come courting couldn't sweet-talk her into anything, and the older men who tried to do more than that went home with bugs in their ears—if they had any ears left enough to hold a bug.

"Nossir, pretty as she was, and set up with a nice farm and a little store that set right here where this one does, she was independent as all get-out. That didn't set too well with the menfolk, as you might imagine, and even the other women, young and old, resented the fact that she could make her own living while they had to put up with their own sorry men in order to keep on eatin'."

Will Henry nodded. He had heard talk among his mother's friends, even in modern times, about women who were not dependent upon men. Even the gentlest ladies seemed to find something really disturbing about that.

"Well, Sir, she got to be about twenty-five, which was old for a woman to be unmarried back then, and instead of witherin' up like a prune she just got prettier and prettier, till the men and the women both just couldn't seem to stand it. And besides that, she took that little old store her granddaddy had built and made it grow and prosper, which it never had done before. The folks back then thought that was really agin nature, for a woman to be so good at business, but there was nothin' they could do. To stop her from gettin' richer, they'd have had to hitch up their teams and take two days to and from Tompkins, and they couldn't spare the time or the energy for that.

"It rocked along, and she bought up more land and put more sharecroppers to work, and her cotton brought top dollar at the compress. Finally, her cousin Mark Convers decided he just had to take her down off her high horse. He wrote back East, where he'd gone to college, and invited his friend Robert Ables to come for a visit.

"He knowed for sure that Robert was rich and handsome and a woman killer from the word go. He'd just barely escaped a couple of shotgun weddings back in New England, where he came from, and there was a trail of broke hearts all around the college where they'd gone to school. Robert, he figured, was just the one to break Malissa to the halter and take her down a whole lot of pegs in the process.

"After a few months, up rode Robert Ables on his sorrel mare, dressed up fit to kill, even after travelin' all the way down the Wilderness Road, taking the Cumberland River to Nashville, and catchin' the Natchez Trace to where it hooked up with El Camino Real, and that was a sight farther then than it is now, let me tell you." Sol tucked a pinch of tobacco in his cheek and waited for it to settle down.

"And did he? Take her down a peg?" asked Chuck. He had a sneaking sympathy for anyone who thought that girls were uppity.

"Not exactly. That sweet-talking S.O.B. took one look at Malissa and was lost. He was so took with her that he paid no heed to all the other young women around that was tryin' their best to ketch his eye. He followed her around like a puppy dog till she run him off and told him not even to come to the store. He could visit her at home, on Sunday, but no place and no time else.

"Which put him right in the path of Patrick Germany, who had made up his mind to marry Malissa or die. Turned out, of course, he died, but that was some later and a lot of grief had flowed under the bridge by then.

"Malissa hadn't much patience with folks of any sort, but some less than that with calf-eyed menfolk. She'd run Pat off most a year before Robert came on the scene, but he kept hangin' around her, when he could. And he took instant dislike to Robert, being as Pat was as country as a hickory nut. So even though she hadn't give the time of day to either of 'em, they begun bowing up at each other like two tomcats."

Will Henry hadn't a romantic bone in his body, and he was getting tired of all this stuff about jealousy and pretty girls. "So what happened?" he asked, his tone bored.

Sol glanced at him from beneath his bushy brows. "Oh, they kilt each other."

Will Henry choked on a fresh gulp of strawberry, and Chuck straightened suddenly. "Malissa went to a church social—the kind where the gals take a basket lunch, and the men bid on it and the highest bidder gets to eat that lunch with the gal what packed it. She wasn't much of a hand to cook, but her old Mandy Lee was, and it wasn't just the woman that attracted all the bids. Everybody knowed he'd get his money's worth, no matter how much that lunch cost him.

"Robert was the richest, of course, and he outbid ever'body. Pat near swallowed his tongue, my grandpa said, when them two went off to set together in the arbor and eat. Unfortunately for everybody concerned, Robert seemed to think his bid had bought him more than just food and the lady's company.

"First thing you knowed, there come a yell and a whack from the arbor, and Robert come running out, with Malissa right behind him, hittin' him with the empty basket. "That was too much for old Pat. He run home through the woods and got his shotgun, and when he got back, he blowed Robert to Kingdom Come, but not before Robert got his hogleg pistol out of his pocket and shot Pat up pretty bad, too.

"Well, there was women screaming and men cussing and kids cryin' all over the place. Malissa taken one look at Robert and said, "Cover him up. He's dead," just as cool as could be.

"She checked out Pat and sent for the doctor, but she shook her head like she hadn't much hope. She didn't look a bit sad about either of 'em, either. Grandpa said the women blamed her pretty harsh for that."

"But what about the baby? And the grave being out in the woods?" asked Will Henry, who liked this sort of tale much better than any love story.

"Just hold on, I'm gettin' there," grunted Sol. "Robert was buried up in Kingdom Come Cemetery, which was pretty small and almost full by then. And in a little bit, Pat died of his wounds and they planted him right there beside Robert.

"Mark had a tombstone cut and put over the man's grave, seein' as he was only there because of Mark and all, and when Pat got planted he hadn't no stone at all. Nobody volunteered to have one made, either.

"Which should have been all right. But Pat wasn't dead. Not quite. Somebody went up there to do some work on a family grave, and there was Pat, who'd dug hisself out of his own hole and was diggin' away at Robert's grave-mound with his bare hands."

Will Henry gave a delicious shiver, which he felt echoed in

Chuck's elbow against his side. This was even better than shooting and sudden death.

"Well, you can imagine what sort of a start that give the one what found him. But he got Pat back down to the settlement and called the doctor, who was pretty put out that his diagnosis had been wrong. But in a while, old Pat died agin, and they put him right back where he was.

"And about that time, little Tildy Jenkins found out she was in the family way, and when her Pa got the truth out of her it turned out that Robert hadn't entirely ignored all the girls that made eyes at him. Tildy was goin' to have Robert's baby, and Robert was cold in his grave and couldn't make a honest woman of her. Her Pa turned her out of the house, and Malissa took her in and let her help in the store.

"Well, Pat was under ground, and Robert was out of it, and things should have settled down a bit. But old Pat, he must of been the toughest character ever born in Cotton County, for up he come agin and they found him diggin' after Robert in the bald sunshine in the middle of the day.

"And that was just a bit too much. Malissa stood up in meeting the next Sunday, after Pat had died agin and been buried agin, and volunteered to give a patch of ground if the menfolk would move Robert. "Does a man who'd betray a girl while he dangled after another woman, and then die and leave her alone with her problem, deserve to lie in hallowed ground?" That was how Grandpa quoted her, though he may have flowered it up some."

"Oh," said Will Henry. "And it was out in the woods?"

"'T'wasn't woods then. Not big woods, anyways. Just new growth, where they'd let some of the tilled land go fallow. They got the preacher to say some words over the spot to make a tiny little cemetery out of it, and when Tildy's baby died, before it hardly got started growin', they put it right there beside its daddy. Felt like it was sort of fittin'.

"And they made a big old iron cage, and they drove stakes down around Pat's grave and fastened it to them, so if he ever taken it into his head to come to life agin and go lookin' for Robert Ables, there was no way on God's green earth he could get out and do it."

The boys' eyes were saucer-round. "You mean that? They caged him down in his grave?" asked Will Henry in a hushed voice. The thought was overwhelming.

"They did. And if you kin get your Pa to take you up over Flowery Mountain to Kingdom Come Cemetery, it's still there. I was up there a year or so ago, when my family had a graveyard workin'. The iron is rusty as all get-out, but it's still there, and old Pat never got out, even if he might've dug up to the surface agin. Which I devoutly hope he didn't. It don't do to think too hard about bein' buried alive, let me tell you."

Will Henry gulped, feeling his strawberry pop lie heavy in his stomach. The thought of being under there, alive, in the dark—and with a sturdy cage waiting, if you managed to get up to daylight— just about turned him wrong-side out.

He rose, a bit shakily. "You fellows comin' with me?" he asked his assembled chums. "We got work to do."

After such a tale as that, thinking and planning about catching a giant catfish looked like a lead-pipe cinch.

XVII.

COW IN THE CANE FIELD

Will Henry was getting really antsy about catching Grampa Catfish. Here it was late September, and they had hardly done more than eliminate a couple of the ways the job might have been done. They were down to poisoning the water with rotenone, just about, because every time they asked Uncle Sol about something like telephoning for fish or suchlike, he had a real horror story that got it marked off the list.

That method was illegal, now, of course, but it hadn't always been, and Tim found to his joy that his Uncle Zeke had some of the stuff in a syrup bucket in his Grandmama's shed. He found it by accident and asked what that powdery stuff was, and Zeke, who never had married and hung around to live off Grandmama's Social Security check, remembered what it was, after a bit.

Tim was as smart as they came, and he just nodded and said, "I wondered. I thought it might be fertilizer we could use for Ma's pea patch. Too bad it's just poison." But he didn't fail to report the find to his chief, and Will Henry began to plan hard.

They'd decided on a pool near the outlet of the channel between Catfish Lake and the river. They'd even gone down and dug out the sides to be straight, instead of uneven, so they could fit a barrier into it securely. But the weather turned nasty on them, with a hurricane coming in off the coast and rains fit to drown them standing straight up.

There was no way they could get down to the river in weather like that, so they spent their Saturday perched like a line of jaybirds on the edge of Mrs. Bragg's porch. Of course, that put them right in the way of Uncle Sol's tales, which made up a little for the rain and wind that bent the pines over in long bows and spun broken-off twigs and sweet gum balls at the porch, from time to time.

It was the middle of the afternoon, gray and gloomy and damp. The overhang of the porch roof ran a sheet of water that splashed into that standing on the ground below, and the spray was rather a nice tickle against Will Henry's ankles. He was sipping a strawberry pop with less enthusiasm than usual when a long black Lincoln pulled up and stopped by the store.

It was about the third limousine that Will Henry had seen in all his life, and the other two had been in Tompkins. Nobody in the river-bottom country could afford a second-hand Chevy, hardly, much less a plush car like the one now standing sublimely indifferent to the rain, as a man in a uniform got out and raised a big shiny umbrella before opening the back door and helping out a tiny little woman in a bright red pantsuit.

The pair proceeded to climb the steps onto the porch, shake out the umbrella, at least the driver did, and then he held the door open so the woman could go inside. There came a feminine shriek of surprise and delight. It took a minute for Will Henry to understand that it was Mrs. Bragg making all the noise...he had never heard her do anything but make gruff statements and boom orders to salesmen and Uncle Sol.

"Who in the world is that?" he asked the old man.

Sol's blue eyes almost sank in the wrinkles around them as he grinned. "Miss Mattie Pike, she was. Name's Cottingham, now. She lives down on the coast, and I 'spect the storm brought her up home to get out of its way. Lord, I can still see that woman runnin' through that cane field...." He broke into a torrent of chuckles that threatened to topple him, chair and all, out into the rain.

The boys turned with military precision to face him. "What cane field?" asked Chuck, feigning indifference, as he turned up his bottle for another sip.

Sol glanced back at the wall of the store as if to gauge its thickness and sound-proofing. Then he started to laugh again, and that decided him. Let the consequences fall as they might, he had a hot story just begging to be told.

"Well, you got to know that Miss Mattie Pike was the daughter of one of the biggest land-holders in Cotton County. They wasn't rich, mind you. Hadn't no money at all, except when they sold their cotton and syrup. They had bottom- land along the Nichayac, and what was too wet for cotton was just right for sugarcane.

"Her Pa was old Mattson Pike, a tall skinny old coot that could pick cotton with the best of 'em and swing a cane knife that would take a whole stool of cane stalks with one whack. And Miss Mattie was maybe the size of Fane here, and she could most near keep up with him. Her Ma died when she was born, and her Pa just learned her to be a boy, which he needed, instead of a girl, which he didn't."

The door opened, and Sol tactfully cut off his story and rolled his snuff around his jaw as the little woman and her large escort left the store and departed in the silent and arrogant car. He spat into the rain after it, but not in an insulting way.

"That gal yonder could outwork most four men, when she got goin'. Used to work in the hayfields, too. We've baled many a bale of hay together, her'n me and the hands. She's maybe four or five years younger'n me, but she hit the ground workin', seems as if. Never saw nobody, except for Slewfoot Sally, that seemed so dead in love with work.

"So when her Pa hired him a man to oversee the whole farm, once they got so they had a little spare cash, it just taken the wind out of her sails. She hated the very notion of housework, but if that was all there was to do, then by golly she set in to do it better'n anybody before or since. She made a garden that could of fed most of Cotton County, and then she turned around and canned every last bean and pea and tomato or whatnot she could find in it.

"And woe betide anybody or anything that interrupted her. No matter how hot and sticky it got, come June and July when her stuff was coming off, she kept right at it till she had the last jar sealed tight as Dick's hatband."

He started chuckling again, joggling his rolls of fat gently. "I was working in their hay, that summer, with William. Yale'd gone off to Tompkins and was workin' in the compress, by that time. Miss Mattie was maybe fifteen and as big as she was ever goin' to get. We was balin' right up close to the fence around the yard, and on down a piece was the cane field she kept for her own syrup for the house.

"About the time we knocked off to go to the water jug and a bite of lunch, I looked over at the house and saw her come flying out, her shirt-tail poppin' in the breeze. She was lookin' off toward the cane field, and when I turned I could see a pretty little Jersey heifer just strolling through the cane, trompling down what she pleased and chewin' on the rest.

"Well, I'd eased myself up to go and help her, but believe me there wasn't time. Miss Mattie'd picked up a hammer, someplace as she came, and she whizzed into that field and took after that cow like a streak of lightnin'. The Jersey, she looked up and took a gander at what was coming at her, and she begun to run round and round, as if she couldn't find the hole in the fence she'd come through. Finally, she give a leap like one of these here jumping horses and cleared that fence as pretty as you please." He sighed.

"So we went back to baling hay, and I most forgot about that cow. But the next time I looked over at the house, by gum that cow was right back in the cane, and Miss Mattie was sailing off again to run her out. And I could see the smoke coming out of the kitchen stovepipe and knowed she had jars in the canner and hated like poison to leave 'em unsupervised.

"Four times she had to run that cow out, and the last time I just stopped and watched, and the other hands did, too, because if ever I seen blood in any woman's eye, it was in Miss Mattie's. Her face was red as a tomato, and she had a look to her like a bee that's decided to sting somebody and don't much care who.

"The Jersey watched her coming with that smug look they can get sometimes when they think they've got some pore human outwitted. She started to trot, little prancy steps, and got to the fence. Then she swung wide, like she was going to flank Miss Mattie, and that was her big mistake.

"Miss Mattie swung back her arm and let fly with that hammer and hit that cow right between the eyes. Now a hammer isn't something you ever want to get hit with. It's heavy, to begin with, and when it's swung or flung—or both, as in this case—it packs a mean wallop.

"That cow went down as if she'd been poleaxed. I run to the fence, and the other men with me, and we could see that animal's eyes rolled right up into her head, showing nothin' but whites. We thought sure she was dead as a doorknob.

"Miss Mattie walked over and picked up her hammer. She leaned over and looked close at the cow. Then she kicked her in the side, not hard, just enough to show she meant business.

"That Jersey rolled her eyes back down, looked up at Miss Mattie, and got up right quick. She run hard as she could to the hole she'd made in the fence to begin with, and if a cow had hands she'd have patched it after she got through to the other side.

"And Miss Mattie never had to run her out of the patch no more. Even after the cane was cut and the other cows got turned into the remainders, old Buttercup wouldn't go into it or even around it. Which proves that even a cow can learn pretty good, if you show 'em you mean business."

That was the sort of tale Will Henry liked. But he had a question. "So how'd Miss Mattie get so rich?" he asked. "Nobody but rich folks can drive a Lincoln Continental, with a driver and all."

Sol cocked a bright eye at him. "Anybody with that much

gumption can do anything she damn well pleases," he said. "She married James Cottingham, which was the fellow her Pa had hired to run the place, and they made things hum. Put in a couple of oil wells, when the boom come, and then they had money to burn. Now they've got all the old family land up here, a house on the coast, a couple more in Florida and Oregon, and Lord knows what else.

"And if anybody on earth ever earned a high-heeled good time, it was Miss Mattie Pike. She done more work before she was twenty than most folks do in a long lifetime."

There came a heavy gust of wind that spattered rain back onto the porch-sitters. Will Henry scootched back against the wall with Chuck and Tim and Les and Fane. Sol's bulk sheltered them all comfortably, as they stared up the road, thinking of that long black car and the tiny red-clad woman inside who had knocked a cow out cold.

It was a pretty mind-boggling thought.

XVIII.

BATTLE PLAN NUMBER ONE

Will Henry wasn't a boy to forget a plan, no matter how much time or how many interruptions got in his way. When he set his mind on something, Tim and Chuck and the little boys had come to understand that it was going to happen, sooner or later.

School, of course, was a big obstacle, when you needed to spend time in the swamp studying how to go about catching the big cat. The necessity for keeping their movements secret didn't help a bit, but they all knew that any parent learning of their trips into the swamp would put the kibosh on them immediately.

So when a teachers' work-day came on a Friday, leaving them a long weekend to play with, it seemed to Will Henry that his chance had come. He told Tim to get a plastic bag of rotenone out of the can in his grandfather's shed. He told Chuck to ask his Mama if he could sleep over at the Emersons' on Friday night.

Tim and his brothers managed to use the visit of a bunch of cousins and aunts and uncles as an excuse for a camp-out in the woods, to make room for all the extra people and pallets and cot-beds. Their mother thought that was a very nice and thoughtful thing for them to do, and they took the credit, grinning, and didn't tell her anything more.

For once, the lawn was mowed, the walks swept, the garbage disposed of, and Will Henry's mother couldn't find anything extra for the boys to do before they set off for the woods. That meant that the two passed Mrs. Bragg's before even Uncle Sol had put in his appearance, crossed the fence into the cornfield leading past the shed that housed the Great Alligator, and slid into the forest so early that the mist was still hanging in the low spots and the owls were still calling their morning hoots.

The three brothers were waiting, their bedrolls neatly tied and stashed beneath a huge hickory, their supplies of sandwiches, line, buckets, rotenone, and hope ready for instant use. Their eyes were wide, their grins wider, and they fell in behind Will Henry with military precision, as Chuck brought up the rear and they all headed off into Sundown Swamp, cutting toward the outflow into the river.

The squirrels were careering through the hickory and oak trees, dropping nuts and acorns, flirting with each other, playing tag up and down the rough bark of the trees and across perilous hanging bridges of grapevine. They were having so much fun that the boys stopped, in spite of themselves, to watch.

But Will Henry, stern taskmaster that he was, came to himself in a few minutes and shook himself like a wet dog. "We've got to get a move on," he said. "We've got to finish digging out a spot to poison, where we can cut off the hole with our net. The big catfish may not be there, right at first, so we'll have to give him time to come to the bait. And then we've got to give the rotenone a chance to work. Sometimes it takes a while, Uncle Sol says."

They darted ahead, and the path was now a familiar thing, even if it was still flanked by muck full of moccasins and pools where alligators eyed them lazily and sinky holes they must avoid, if they were not to sink painfully to their deaths. They knew the places to avoid, and they knew where they were going. Those two things made the trip quick and easy.

The spot they had chosen, weeks before, for their attempt was at the river end of the channel connecting the swamp with the stream. Already they had managed to dredge out a big hole, nibbled into the soft sand along the bank, that seemed large enough to hold a Cadillac, not to mention a catfish. Every time they returned to it, however, there was work to do, for rain and the rising and falling of the water levels washed sand down into it, sloping their straight embankments.

This time was no exception. The hurricane rains that had hit them the week before had brought debris of all kinds, as well, and it took them until noon to get the hole shaped to their satisfaction. While they were working on that, Will Henry, always thinking, had staked the bait, a very dead chicken, out in the current, tying it to a snag of willow. The catfish should come to that, he thought, if he was wandering around downstream.

They had woven a latticework of saplings and covered that with a bit of heavy fishnet they had found caught on a drift beside the river. It wasn't big enough to be any use to a fisherman, but it was just the size they wanted to stop off the entrance to their fish trap. They'd weighted the lower edge with rocks and lead from lost fish lines.

They placed the heavy barrier on the slope of sand above the slot where it was to go, before they stopped long enough to eat the sandwiches they had brought. They could have eaten twice as many again, when those were gone, but Will Henry harried them into action.

Now the chicken was swirling gently in the trap, the outflow carrying the scent, they all hoped, down into the river to attract their prey. While they waited, they positioned themselves so as to move most effectively when the time came. And then they lay flat on their skinny bellies, expecting the behemoth to appear at any moment.

They were full. It was hot beneath the trees, and the steamy breath off the water made them drowsy. One by one, they dozed off, letting their browned cheeks drop onto hands or the sand beneath them. Even Will Henry, Napoleon of schoolboys, went into dreamland.

When he awoke, it was to find himself looking straight down into the pool they had made. Something long and dark was lying there, its tail swishing gently back and forth as it rested after its meal. There was no sign of the chicken anywhere.

The boy tensed. His elbow went out to nudge Tim's side. "Hey! Tim! Wake up! Shove Chuck, will you?"

The other boy's eyes opened, his gaze foggy for a moment. Then he, too looked down. His mouth opened in a silent cry.

He reached out a foot to kick Les, and his hand tweaked Chuck's shoulder. "He's there!" he whispered. "By Johnny Jingo, he's there!"

All five of them rose on hands and knees to peer down into the deep hole. The leaf-shadows and the ripples made it hard to see their catch, but what else of that size could it be? They moved as one, rushing to slip the gate down into the water, securing their catch.

The splash woke the big fish from its after-meal trance. It darted toward the river, only to be baffled by the gate. It swam frantically around and around, as Will Henry measured out rotenone into a Mason jar, added water from the river, and splashed the resultant mixture into the hole.

Again they waited, but this time there was no sleeping on the job. They watched as the fish slowed. Slowed still more. Came to a stop, resting gently against the muddy bottom of the pool...and turned on its side to drift upward as quietly as a dead leaf.

When it reached the surface, five naked boys were there to receive it...and once they got a good look at their prey their faces were filled with disappointment.

"A bass—a dadgummed bass! Wouldn't you know that'd be our luck? All this work for nothing but a bass!" Will Henry sounded as if he might cry.

Tim, however, was staring at the fish that they had now tugged onto the sand and secured with line through its lower jaw. "Will Henry, that's got to be the biggest damn bass I ever seen in all my life," he said, his tone awed. "You look at that thing!"

Will Henry stared down, his mouth closing and then opening again as he realized the size of their catch. The thing had to weigh nearly twenty pounds; it was the most unearthly huge fish of its kind he had ever heard of. Its barrel belly would have been a long stretch for both his arms to reach around, and its mouth could hold the bottom of their water bucket and still leave room for more.

Chuck was gasping with amazement, his eyes round, his cheeks scarlet with emotion. "My Dad caught a ten-pounder, and he most busted his buttons he was so proud. Here we got one that has to weigh fifteen, if it's an ounce, Will Henry. You talk about a monster, this 'uns as big for a bass as Grampa Catfish is for a catfish."

Tim had been walking around and around the thing, measuring it with his eyes. Now he looked up at the two bigger boys. "So how we goin' to say we cotch him? Can't tell anybody how we really done it—and for goodness sake not where we done it! They's no way in the world anybody's goin' to believe we cotch this critter on a hook and line. There's not a rig in Cotton County could hold that fish."

This was a new problem. And it was a valid question. If they let anyone get a hint of what they had been up to, their Great Catfish Hunt would be off for good. No, they had to think up a plausible tale that people might wonder about but would have to accept. Naturally, they all turned to Will Henry, who was good at tales of all sorts.

He sank onto his haunches, watching the bass. Suddenly he realized that the creature was suffocating, and he gestured for the others to help him put it into the water, secured by the line in its jaw. The gills began moving more easily, and the tail began its swishing again.

The boy began to grin. "You know the big hole up near the old Cotton Landing? The one where Uncle Sol's Daddy caught the hundred-pound turtle?"

Chuck nodded, his eyes brightening. He began to smile, too.

"We'll go back that way. They always keep seines drying on the bamboo thicket, off toward the creek. We just might take down a seine to catch some bait, and we just might happen to luck into the biggest bass ever netted out of the river by anybody."

They hung the giant bass on a stick that Will Henry and Chuck, being the tallest, carried over their shoulders to keep his tail from dragging on the ground. The five of them sped up the riverbank to the old landing, where riverboats, back when the river was navigable, brought in goods and took away the cotton from the fields roundabout.

They were in luck. Nobody was in sight.

Not one of the boys liked lying, if there was any alternative, so they took down a seine and dragged it through the shallows up by the bank, and Tim laid the big bass, now just about gone to join his ancestors, in the water to be scooped up and caught anew.

Then, with their legitimized catch over their shoulders, the five headed for Mrs. Bragg's. Uncle Sol was, of course, sitting on the porch, surrounded by Saturday shoppers, a couple of disgruntled fishermen, and a cloud of dust just left by a pickup truck loaded with high school boys.

Someone noticed the approaching group and their burden. Uncle Sol rose ponderously from his chair and stood on the edge of the porch, staring at the fish hanging down between Chuck and Will Henry. Mrs. Bragg, coming onto the porch to fuss at someone for something, turned to see what Sol was looking at and stopped in mid-syllable, her mouth wide open.

It was with the air of conquering heroes returning from the wars that Will Henry's crew swaggered up to the store. "We caught one, Uncle Sol," Will Henry said modestly.

The old man opened and shut his mouth several times, for all the world like a bass himself. Then he said, "I see you did, boy. Biggest damn bass I ever seen, though I've heard of a couple of bigger ones caught. Nothing like that ever come out of our river before, I'd say. Where in tarnation did you ketch him?"

"The old landing. We were seining, and he just seemed to be there. We got him in, but it wasn't easy." And that, thought the boy, was no lie, either.

Mrs. Bragg stumped down the steps. "If you'd like, I'll put him in my cooler, in case you want to have him stuffed. I'd think your daddies would like you to do that. This big a fish is a record, too good a thing just to eat."

Sol nodded. "And, by golly, I'll pay for having it stuffed, if you'll let Mrs. Bragg mount it in the store. This should show those fishermen that there's big stuff in our river, down here. Good advertising for Cotton County in general and Possum Creek in partic'lar."

Will Henry looked about at his fellow conspirators. They all

95

nodded. They knew very well that their fish was the result of deliberate disobedience and that they all deserved a whaling. But if it turned out to be a good thing for the whole town, who were they to argue?

When Will Henry trudged off down the road toward home, alone, for Chuck had to be at home for Sunday School the next day, he felt unaccountably good. His conscience seemed to be clear, which it seldom was. But his ambition was still unsatisfied. Today a twenty-pound bass.

Tomorrow, a three-hundred-pound catfish!

XIX.

THE YOUNGERS

The nights were getting longer and longer. There was no time after school for Will Henry and his bunch to visit the store...not if they got their chores and their homework done. So Saturdays were treasured, and the first Saturday in October came along rainy and gloomy and touched with the first hint of chill.

Even so, the five boys were on the porch before noon, but they found Uncle Sol frowning and spitting his snuff with the velocity of a bullet. Something, it was plain, had the old man riled. Will Henry, being the all-time favorite, was the one to break the uncomfortable silence.

"Uncle Sol, what's wrong? You look like you've got a bellyache," he ventured, touching the old man's knee to get his attention.

The bushy white brows twitched irritably, and the blue eyes focused on the boy, as if they pulled in from gazing a long way into the distance. His glance was so fierce that the boy backed off a bit, startled.

"Them damn Youngers! Been a pain in the ass for near onto sixty years, now, and they don't get no better, and nobody's had the guts to take after 'em and shoot every last one!" Sol snapped. Then he relented and shoved a hand into his pocket for change.

"Here, you go and get you something to drink while I cool down a mite. It's a little chilly for cold drinks, but I recall when I was younger; I could drink a nice cold pop on the coldest day God ever hatched." He doled out money, and the boys filed into the store after their strawberry soda pop, while Mrs. Bragg fixed them with her granite eye to make sure they didn't topple any of her neat pyramids of canned goods.

When they went back out, they all huddled together against the wall of the store, out of the damp breeze. Sol had his jacket shrugged around him, as if, he, too, were cold, once his inner anger died down. His forehead was still furrowed with deep lines.

"Who're the Youngers?" asked Will Henry. "Any kin to old Frank Allen Younger? My Dad used to work for him."

"Different batch," said Sol. "Frank's a decent human being, but that batch over t'other side of the river is sheer poison. As bad, in their way, as the Smiths was. Not killers like the Smiths, but just nasty, destructive hoodlums." Sol was snorting again, his face flushing with anger.

"So what have they done?" asked Will Henry.

"Spent sixty years being the world's worst pests. But last night they went out to my cabin, down on the home place, and did their worst. They even got inside, after all these years of my shutters holdin' 'em out!"

Every one of the boys knew that cabin and loved it. From time to time Sol would invite their entire families to spend a weekend there, and the youngsters looked forward to those weekends with as much enthusiasm (or perhaps more) as they would have shown for a trip to Heaven. So they all sat up straight, forgetting their pop bottles, and turned pale.

"They didn't break the kerosene lamps!" whispered Chuck, who took great delight in spending the nights by the glow of the lamps, which lit the big room of the cabin dimly and yet with wonderful warmth.

"Busted two of 'em. I've got Mrs. Bragg busy orderin' me a half dozen more, just to be on the safe side. They got the ruby red one and the blue glass one. Darn 'em!" Sol's tone was savage, and the boys felt entirely sympathetic.

"What about the bunk beds?" asked Tim. "My brothers and me, we just love to climb up and sleep in that top bunk, right under the ceiling, and hear the flying squirrels moving around up in the attic."

"They burnt the mattress, but they didn't chop up the bunks themselves. For what that's worth."

"The well! They didn't mess up the well and the bathing place with the gunny-sack curtains around it and the old bucket," pleaded Will Henry. "I love to go out and draw water better than most anything. And in summer, it's a pure pleasure to take a bath in the Number Three washtub, even if the water is cold enough to freeze you blue."

"They tore down the shed over the well, and they bent the bucket in about ten places, and they burnt up the gunnysack curtain around the cement floor of the bathing spot," grunted Sol. "And they also burnt up every stick of the winter wood I'd had cut and stacked there for this winter, when somebody wanted to do some cold weather fishing or some bird hunting out there. Dadgum 'em! Cost me forty dollars, and here it is all gone right now, before winter's got started good."

This was shocking news. Several times a year, they could look forward to making a trip out to Sol's home farm and the log cabin. It was like taking a trip back into the past, for there was no electricity, no running water, no indoor plumbing. A trip through the woods at night, by the light of a kerosene lantern, to visit the privy ranked among the high adventures of their young lives.

The path was crooked as a drunk snake, with woods on both sides. There was a screech owl that made its home in a big sweet gum along the way, and its eerie wail was guaranteed to make anyone's hair stand straight up, in the midst of such a trip. Will Henry privately thought that there was no place on earth as far away and as isolated as wherever you happened to be along that path, with the lantern making a circle of light around you, when that owl cut loose. You felt like the last living soul in the world, and the little log privy, a two-holer with a crescent cut in the door, looked like Salvation itself, once you got there.

He leaned back, remembering the distinctive smell of the place, which was a mix of old logs, wasp nests, and years of lime that had made a valiant effort to overcome the natural smell of the pit beneath the holes. Civilization was all right for everyday living, he felt, but for sheer adventure and a feeling that you were on top of things, it took going back to the sort of old-timey doings that Sol's cabin represented.

"And the Youngers have been doing this kind of thing for years? Why haven't we heard about it?" he asked.

"'Cause they stay across the river, that's why. It's just bad luck my old home place is on that side. Even when Yale was still alive and lived there, they used to come and scallyhoot around, tearin' things up and scaring the cattle and just generally raising hell. I almost got 'em, not long after Yale died. Had a right brisk little war, for a while." He chuckled, remembering.

That brought his listeners to attention. They recalled their pop and took big swigs. Then they scooched close around his chair and looked up, not even needing to say that they wanted to hear that tale right now.

Mrs. Bragg came clumping out of the store with a steaming mug in her hands. It was Uncle Sol's LIAR'S AWARD cup, and she handed it to him without a word. But as she went back inside, they heard her mutter, "Crazy old fool...sitting out in the weather in this damp! Get his death of cold!" And then she was gone, and Sol was sipping the hot liquid with satisfaction.

When he was done, his face had regained its natural rosy color, neither pale with rage nor scarlet with fury, and his eyes were beginning to be their usual merry blue, instead of ice-colored. He looked, in fact, ready to tell a story, and the boys settled down to listen.

"Yale died—let me see—must have been in nineteen and sixty-five. He'd lived on the home place, with his wife, and took care of our folks until they died, and William and me agreed he ought to get it. Well, William died of noomony a long time before that, so when Yale went, and his wife said she didn't want the property, just enough money to get her a little place in town and send the kids to school, I was the onliest one left, so I kept it. Couldn't rightly see sellin' my old home."

Will Henry and the other boys nodded. They understood that nobody who owned the land, the woods, the cabin, and the fish-ponds could possibly give them up.

"The house was all but falling down, by then, so I took it all the way down and cut enough logs off the woodlot to build the cabin, which was all I needed. I finished it out with stuff from the other house, and when it was done, I figured I'd made a good job of it." He spat into his snuff can and settled back.

"I'd put it right close to the ponds, so I could fish without having to cross the place, and I dug the well and fixed up the privy and made her shipshape. And then I got shifted over to the other mill in Tompkins, and there was no way it paid me to live way over there and make that long trip twice a day. So I just kept the place for a hideaway, sort of, for me and my friends.

"And that was just the sort of thing them dang Youngers loved to see. They had themselves a high-heeled old time, that first week I was gone. I'd fixed up the shutters and the doors so you mighty near had to tear the place down to get inside, and they hadn't done that, but they'd pushed over the privy and knocked a hole in my boat and burnt up a lot of my firewood and messed things up generally. One thing that always tells you if people are trash is if they don't clean up after theirselves. They don't." Sol shifted in his chair and sighed.

"Well, one night I was dozing in my house in Tompkins, and the phone rang downstairs. Mrs. Slotter come tramping up the stair to tell me somebody called and said I'd better get out to my cabin. The Youngers was all over the place, drunk as lords, and might burn everything down if I didn't stop 'em. It was old Milt Hempstead called...he lived a few miles down the road, then, where the tumble-down remains of a house stand now, you recollect?"

The boys nodded.

"He had a phone, and he rung me up, and I taken out with my britches buttoned all wrong and my shotgun in my hand. I also had my Pa's hogleg revolver stuck in my waistband, because I didn't intend to take nothing off no Youngers, if I had to shoot the everlasting lot of 'em. I had a head of steam on that could have run me through a stone wall, and you'd better believe I made my old Ford fly. I got there about an hour after the call come through, and I stopped the car where the woods begins and parked it.

"I figured there was no use in warning them that somebody was coming, so I injuned through the trees, just as quiet as I could—and back then I was a master hand in the woods, you'd better believe me—and come up on the far side of the cabin, where the little creek runs into the smaller pond." He drew his eyebrows together and looked positively ferocious.

"They was drinking and laying around on my homemade out-door chairs and throwing my logs on a fire they'd built in my flow-erbed. I could see where they'd chopped at the shutters, trying to get into the cabin, but I'd put those suckers up there to stay, and they hadn't had any luck.

"They had little kids running around naked as jaybirds, jumping into the pond in the dark, no matter that there was water moccasins and to spare around it. There was some of their women, drunk as the men and louder, and about ten of the young fellows, just lookin' for trouble.

"Well, I watched for about five minutes. Then I got around into position and I give 'em all they could handle. Y'see, there's an echo, if you yell from just the right angle. Your voice kind of bounces off the big woods off to the north, and it sounds just plain lifelike. So I taken a big breath and I yelled, 'Get 'em, boys! Shoot the boogers!'

"Then I let loose with the shotgun, first one barrel and then the other, and the yells and the booms come rumblin' back from the other side, and all the Youngers jumps up or lays down or runs around till it looks like a chicken pen when a hawk flies over. I re-loaded and let off a couple of rounds into the hickory trees in the yard, and twigs and bark come raining down on 'em, and they knowed for sure and certain they was shot dead." Sol began to laugh.

"They started pilin' into their old pickups and cars, which was parked everwhichaways on my shrubbery and flowerbeds, little na-ked kids and drunk women and old men and young men until it looked like Bedlam, sure enough. I kept encouragin' 'em with a round, one time the shotgun, next time the handgun, just peppering the life out of the tops of the trees. Once they got everybody they could locate into the cars, they shot off like crazy people, tearing off through the woods and just catching the road from time to time.

"I could hear a crash, now and again, when one of 'em would run over a good-sized sapling or into a tree. They come in five cars, but they only got out with three, for the other two was smashed up in my woods, beyond repair, if they'd been worth repairin' in the first place. Which they wasn't." Sol began to chuckle again.

"Well, I went up to the cabin and stomped out the fires and wet 'em down, so the woods wouldn't catch. And then I sat down and laughed myself silly. And while I was laughin', I heard something in the darkness around the other side of the cabin. Once I got my flashlight around there, I found one of them little kids, still naked, lying in the honeysuckle vines, just cryin' her heart out. They'd went off and left her.

"And that was a problem for me. I purely hated to take that young'un back and hand her over to them wild-eyed idiots, but what else could I do? And I didn't want anybody to know it was me that broke up their little party, either. So I taken her to Milt, and asked if he'd make out like he'd found her in the woods, all alone, and brought her home.

"She was too scared to know who was who or what was what, but she did know her name, and he said he'd take care of it. So the little one got took home, and I saved the cabin, which I feel sure would have burned up then and there, and the Youngers never knowed it was me. That put a scare into 'em that lasted for years, till the new crop of 'em come on that didn't recall anything about it. But now they're back again, and I'm too damned old to go skyrocketin' through the woods and shooting up the landscape, nowadays. It's a real shame."

Will Henry was wide-eyed, Chuck pale with interest, and Tim and his brothers leaning forward intently. Every one of them knew the value of that rough cabin. They all realized that their fathers would rush to its defense.

Will Henry said, "Uncle Sol, is there anybody out there that could phone you a warning, since Old Milt is dead?"

Sol looked up. "Why, I guess Miss Sarah Brewster could. She lives along the road to the old place. Why?"

"Well, you just ask her to let you know if they go by toward your cabin. I'll bet my Dad would take off like a shot, if you called him. And Chuck's too."

"And mine, too," piped up Les. Fane and Tim nodded.

Sol began to smile, a wide grin that lighted up the gray day and seemed to warm away the chill. "I might just do that," he said.

The boys sighed. Some things were worth fighting for, their dads had told them all. And this, they knew very well, was one of the most important of them.

XX.

YALE'S WEDDING

Chuck's older sister, Marilyn, got engaged on the first Sunday in October. This puzzled Chuck and his friends quite a lot—not, of course, that Marilyn would want to marry but why a neat guy like Charles Wallington would want to entangle his life with a girl. They couldn't but feel that it was going to put a real hitch into his fishing and hunting.

It was almost an entire week before they could lay the matter in the ample lap of Solomon Peat, who had hitched his hickory splint chair over into the corner of the porch, where the wall of the store would shelter him from the chilly fall wind. They found him with his Liar's Award mug between his hands, sipping Mrs. Bragg's strong brew and waiting for their arrival.

"Hear your big Sis is getting married!" he greeted Chuck. "Sort of young, ain't she, for such a step? Charlie's at least six years older than she is."

Chuck shrugged, being without any answer to the question, and held out his hand for the pop-money. Will Henry, feeling left out and unimportant, which was a thing he had little experience with, led the troop of boys into the store and out again with their red bottles.

Sol was talking with Mittie Leggett, when they got back, and they dropped onto the floor and leaned against the wall, waiting for her to leave. But they found themselves strangely intrigued by her conversation with their old friend. She hinted at matters they had never found interesting enough to pursue, and her sly looks at them, her head-shakings, and her expression told them she was talking around things that people their age shouldn't hear. That, of course, meant they wanted desperately to hear them.

"Well, Sol, I just hope it isn't one of those cases. You know what I mean. I'll be counting the months, you'd better believe, but Jim and Sarah just ran off and got married too soon to sound natural. Her mother will be mortified if anything happens too soon." She sighed dramatically and stumped down the steps, her bunch of fall greens waving like a banner over her shoulder.

Sol spat into his snuff can and put the lid on with unnecessary vigor. "Ain't been a soul born in Cotton County in forty years that that old biddy hasn't counted off on her fingers, hoping like crazy that they'd come enough too soon so as to give her something to wag her tongue about. Jim and Sarah didn't want a church wedding, and all the guests and the fuss and the bother. They'd been living together for two years, anyways. Godamighty! Her ma wanted her to wear white, if you can believe such a thing!"

Will Henry knew there was something important embedded in this pronouncement, but he found himself at sea. Marriage meant babies, that was clear from his own observations. Babies took a certain amount of time to arrive, as he had noted in the case of his Aunt Laura's children. But there was a large gap in his knowledge, and he knew Uncle Sol would fill it.

"Uncle Sol, what was she talking about, anyway?"

Tim snickered, and the boy suddenly realized that he might well have asked him. Black children seemed to pick up on such things more quickly than he seemed to do. But it was too late, for Uncle Sol took the last sip of coffee, turning the mug skyward, and put on his storytelling face.

"Boys," he began, "it's folks like Mittie that make most of the trouble in the world. Young folks just naturally seems to have to get out and canoodle around with each other, which sometimes leads to young'uns that get here a bit quicker than her kind thinks is proper. Nine months is nine months, and let a baby come two weeks early, whatever the truth of the matter, and they snicker and whisper and make snide remarks.

"You take Chuck's sister. That Marilyn is so shy and so neat and so anxious to do the right thing that nobody in his sane senses would think she'd do anything she thought was wrong. But once she and Charles get married, old Mittie is goin' to start counting on her fingers. She'll feel as if there's some hope until they pass the nine-month mark, and then she'll shake her head and go off to start countin' on somebody else. It's her sort that drove old George off to Canada."

"George? George who?" asked Will Henry.

"Why, my cousin George Slocum. He'd be—why, by golly, old George'd be over eighty, now, if he's still alive. Which I haven't a clue of, being as he never wrote nor called after he run off to Canada."

"But why did he run off? Did he...break the law?" asked the boy.

"Not the legal law, no," said the old man. "But the Law According to Mittie Leggett and her sort, yes indeedy. You want to hear the tale? It's too chilly for you to mess around in the woods, today."

All five nodded their heads, sloshing the contents of their pop bottles considerably in the process. Sol folded his arms over his belly and looked off, as he usually did when he was peering into the past.

"Long about nineteen and twenty-seven, when I was mighty near a youngster, still, my brother Yale decided he wanted to get married. He picked out a pretty little thing named Nancy Rossiter, who was visitin' her grandmother in Possum Creek, and he asked her and she said yes. She wasn't from Cotton County at all, being from over in central Texas in the dry country, and we all had to get in the Model T and drive all that way for the wedding. William and Yale and Mama and Pa and me all scrunched up in that car and set off together.

"The baggage was tied on anywhere we could find to tie it, and Yale's good suit was in my lap in the kind of long heavy paper bag the cleaners used to use before there was such a thing as plastic.

"It was a long old trip, back then, for the roads was nothing to speak of and the cars didn't go fast, if they had of been. Time we spent the night in Palestine and rode most of the next day, we was pretty stiff and wrinkled, you'd better believe. But Ma said she could flat-iron our clothes and a good night's sleep would fix us right up, so we'd do the family proud for the wedding."

He sighed and reached for his mug, for he heard Mrs. Bragg's heavy steps coming from the store as she brought the coffee-pot. A good gulp of coffee lubricated his tongue, and he started off again.

"Nancy's folks was what you might call well to do, back then. That meant they owned their house and a new Packard, and her old man had his own hardware store. They wasn't much thrilled with us, but they liked Yale and they knowed that honest poor folks is at least as good as crooked rich ones. So they done the best they could to look happy, and we all got dressed up the next morning for the wedding, which was to be at two.

"Along about noon, a buggy come tearing along the road and pulled up in the lane around behind the house. The horse was near lamed, it had been drove so hard, and the buggy's wheels was almost wore down to a nub. Out of that rig stepped George, and he looked like somebody that'd tangled with a bobcat. He was dusty and ragged and dead beat, but the worst thing was he looked plumb scared to death.

"Mr. and Mrs. Rossiter didn't know what to think, with a perfect stranger busting in that way, just before the wedding...well, not more than a couple of hours before, if that. But Ma, she explained that this was our cousin's boy, and said she'd find out what the matter was, if everybody would just go about their business and give her time.

"Old George had took the horse loose from the buggy and put him in the Rossiters' barn, along with their Packard, and he'd run the buggy back in some brush so's it didn't show from the road at all. That told us all that there was more in the wind than just a sudden whim to go to his cousin's wedding. And Ma, once she talked to him for a while, come back looking pretty grim."

Sol smiled. "Ma was a good woman, but she had a open mind, not like the Mittie Leggetts of the world. She knowed that folks makes mistakes. Lord knows, we was enough to teach her that. She didn't beat around the bush a bit.

"'George has got Mary Scott pregnant. He has the good sense not to want to go through life saddled with a complete idiot, so he took off the minute he heard that her Pa and her brothers was looking for him with shotguns. He don't want to die, but he surely don't want to spend his life with that ninny. He's come to us, and we'd better help him out before two o'clock, because he says the Scotts are probably hot on his heels'." Sol was chuckling, now, his gaze turned inward to see that long-past time.

"Pa headed for the railway station and bought George a ticket. Ma whipped out her sewing basket and tried to put his jacket and pants to rights, but he'd run off through a blackberry thicket, in the beginning, and nothing could be done. I give him my next-best clothes, that I intended to wear on the ride back home, and had to go all the way in my wool suit that most itched the hide off me.

"We got him on the one o'clock train, just by the skin of our teeth, and then we thought we had things nailed down and ready to go. Only we didn't reckon with the Scotts, who come whoopin' and hollerin' into the middle of the wedding, which was in the garden out back of the Rossiters' house.

"The preacher dropped his Bible and hid behind the trellis, and Nancy fainted, and Yale turned pale and lost his temper, when them ring-tailed varmints come riding right through the hedges and over the guests."

Will Henry and Chuck and Tim and the little boys were listening, mouths open, pop forgotten in their hands. This was the best wedding they'd ever heard tell of, and they didn't intend to miss a syllable.

"Old man Rossiter might wear a suit and tie every day of his life and set in a hardware store instead of working in the fields or the woods, but he was a tough customer, any way you slice it. He dashed into his house and come out in just a second with a double-barreled shotgun in his hands. He peppered the Scotts' horses till they reared up and most dumped their riders on the ground. Then they taken off back down the road, and I don't know but they didn't stop till they was back in East Texas."

"So Yale and Nancy went ahead and got married?" asked Chuck, obscurely disappointed at such a tame ending to such a rip-roaring tale.

"Not a bit of it," said Sol. "When Nancy come to and her mother apologized to the guests, while Mr. Rossiter cleaned his shotgun and put it away, and Yale looked the situation over, it just seemed as if everybody agreed that they'd made a mistake. Nancy never could have felt safe in East Texas, that was for sure and certain, and Yale never could have felt at home where there wasn't big old trees and rivers full of catfish. Like Ma said, young love sometimes makes suckers out of people. This time, old George brought 'em back to themselves before they'd gone too far.

"So we tucked ourselves back into the Model T and headed for home again, and somehow even Yale felt better about things than he had when we came. And old George must of gone clear to Canada, like he said he was going to, because we never heard another word of him from that day to this."

Chuck sighed. "I wish old Marilyn would have that kind of wedding," he said. "That would be something to see! But I'll bet she'll have it in the church, and I'll have to go an extra time for it and wear a suit and tie, and it'll be just as prim and proper as she is. Doggone it! Looks as if when sisters got passed out, I got a real dud."

Will Henry, sisterless and glad of it, patted his shoulder. "You can't do a thing about it," he said. "So let's think of something interesting to do to liven things up, when the big day comes. I'll bet old Charles would like to see something out of the ordinary at his wedding."

Solomon Peat opened his mouth. His eyes widened with protest...and then he sank back into his chair, closed his mouth and grinned. Charles might not want to see something out of the ordinary at his own wedding, but Solomon was always game for any excitement going. And he knew those boys.

They'd come up with something choice.

XXI.

GHOST LARRY

Winter had come booming in on the back of a norther, and Mrs. Bragg's porch was just too cold for sitting. Solomon retreated to his winter quarters on the back-side of the big gas heater that filled the store with fumes and heat in about equal quantities. Around him were six splint-bottomed chairs in which the other winter loiterers could sit to hear his tales.

Though Mrs. Bragg grumbled mightily, Will Henry often caught her bending her earringed ear toward the sound of the old man's voice as he took off on one of his accounts. He had to admit that Mrs. Bragg didn't discriminate against you just because you were a youngster...when she got tired of anybody's hanging around inside the store, she sent them packing. As often as not, it was one of the adults who got the boot.

That day it was Larry Wright. As the hunched figure limped out of the door, Solomon began to chuckle. "Did you ever hear the tale about how old Larry got to be called Ghost Larry?" he asked Mrs. Bragg.

She looked disapproving, but she shook her head, setting the earrings to winking in the light. "Can't say as I have," she admitted, her tone grudgingly interested.

"That's a tale I most forgot until I watched him go gimpin' away, just now. You may not know that he was married to Myrtie Finch, over to Flowery Mountain. Way back, that was, when she was just a kid of thirteen or so, and he was maybe twenty-five. He sort of traded her folks out of her, and she had no say in the matter. But she had spunk, even then."

"You mean her folks made a child that age get married? What on earth were they thinking about?" Mrs. Bragg demanded, as she weighed out a pound of shingle nails and sealed them into a bag for

Cooter Scoggins, who always waited until the winter wind sent his roof into shock before he bothered to nail down the loose shingles.

"Ghost Larry's Daddy owned the mill where old man Skinner, her dad, worked. Larry dropped a few hints as to how anybody who didn't do what he said might lose his job. Well, that was in the Depression, and jobs was scarce as hens' teeth, and Skinner had about eleven young'uns to feed. When Larry said he wanted Myrtie, by golly, her daddy said, 'Take her!'

"So that poor little kid got married and moved in with Larry and his daddy, who was a close-mouthed fellow who hated anybody who talked. And Myrtie was a talker, there's no doubt about that."

"Nothing's changed in that department, over the years," murmured Mrs. Bragg, as if to herself.

"She still talks, sure enough. And she still has the guts to take things in hand, the way she did as soon as she realized that her folks had no right to sell her and her husband had no right to buy her. She walked thirteen miles into town, the minute she turned fourteen, and filed charges at the courthouse against the Wrights. She didn't file against her folks, because she knew how hard-run they were and that her daddy was desperate when he gave her to Larry.

"Instead of taking the thing to court, the Wrights settled with the lawyer the District Attorney found for the kid. Gave her an annulment. Gave her enough money to keep her till she got out of school. And she moved back home and helped with the littler kids and shot through the little old school out at Elm Flats like a skyrocket."

"She always was bright," Mrs. Bragg said. "She was the best teacher the Tompkins school ever had, somebody told me."

"Right on the button," Sol said. "And in time she met a man named Finch and he courted her for about three years, until she was certain sure what she was getting into that time, and married him. They had about five children, I think, and she brought 'em up by the book, let me tell you.

"Well, things got a little easier and the Depression let up a bit as the War come on. Carl Finch was too old to draft, but somebody on the draft board had a son the right age, and he was castin' around real desperate for a substitute; he grabbed onto Finch, thirty-eight years old with five kids, and drafted him so's the no-count twenty-one-year-old could stay home and chase girls."

"Happened more than once," said Mrs. Bragg. "My own first cousin got sent to the Pacific and killed, and that left three children to be raised by their mama, who hadn't a bit more than her share of sense and maybe some less."

Sol nodded. "A lot of rich bums got passed over, and a lot of over-age men with families went off to war. And quite a few didn't make it back. Carl Finch made it, but he was so shot up that he spent the rest of his life in a Veterans' Hospital. And poor Myrtie went back to teaching and raised those kids, still by the book, and every one of 'em turned out top-notch."

"But what about Ghost Larry?" asked Chuck, disappointed that the story seemed to be dwindling away into adult nonsense.

"Oh, that happened after the war. Myrtie and her two youngest, who were still in elementary school, came home one evening after getting groceries and such. They lived in a big old house on Plum Street, there in Tompkins, two-storied and high-ceilinged, like they used to build 'em. They never locked their front door—or their back door, for that matter—because in that day and age nobody needed to in East Texas.

"They unloaded Myrtie's old Plymouth and put the groceries away before they went in the front to go upstairs and wash up and change clothes. And there, standing at the head of the stairs, was a white shape.

"Pattie, Myrtie's youngest, told me about it, and she still shivered when she described that wavery figure, waving floaty arms over its head and moaning, 'Ohhhhh, Myrtie! Ohhhh, Myrtie!' like a lost soul."

Will Henry shivered, himself, and he felt Chuck, up against him as they sat in the same chair, quivering, too.

"Well, Myrtie Finch had stood fast and looked a lot of nasty things dead in the eye, and she wasn't going to be shook up by any ghost. She pulled her old revolver out of the desk drawer in the living room, came back into the entrance hall, and shot that white-sheeted critter." He shifted his bulk in the less familiar chair and sighed.

Mrs. Bragg was frankly absorbed in the tale, by this time, leaning on the counter on her elbows, her eyes bright with interest. "And that was...."

"Don't go getting ahead of the story," Sol chided her. "The 'ghost' came tumbling down the stairs, thumping and bumping and trailin' sheet after it, until it arrived in a tangle at her feet. The kids was all having hysterics, because they wasn't used to their mother having to shoot ghosts off the staircase on an ordinary Tuesday afternoon. There was blood seeping into the carpet, and Myrtie was white-mad when she jerked the sheet off and saw that the ghost was old Larry, who she'd done her best to forget about for the past twenty years."

Mrs. Bragg nodded, as if she'd known that all along.

Sol frowned as he went on, "The kids, of course, didn't even know their mama'd been wed before, and she had to explain to them while the police was coming. Larry was moaning and groaning and cursing, till she thumped his head, and she wasn't a bit happy about the whole entire affair.

"So they hauled Larry off to the hospital, and it was only because of his daddy that he didn't go to jail. Myrtie never had a bit of trouble with anybody prowling her house, after the word got out about her shooting, either. She'd hit Larry right in the knee, which is the most painful wound you can get that won't wind up killin' you altogether.

"He's had a stiff knee ever since, and he goes limping around Tompkins, or around Possum Creek when he's out here at his hunting camp, and everybody who remembers the old days calls him Ghost Larry, which doesn't make him a bit happy."

Will Henry incautiously gulped the last of his strawberry pop, and Mrs. Bragg fixed him with her granite eye. "Only customers can sit here for long. You boys get along home, now. You been taking up space for too long."

Sol winked at the pair as they edged out of the cramped spot behind the stove. Will Henry winked back, as he and Chuck pulled on their jackets and their wool caps and stuck their hands in their pockets. The wind outside would cut you off at the knees.

Mrs. Bragg opened the door for them, so their hands could keep the warm from the stove, and Will Henry thanked her politely. But, as he and Chuck went their separate ways, each of them tried limping the way Ghost Larry did, and each of them privately decided never to play ghost for an ex-wife. Particularly one who was a crack shot.

XXII.

The Year the Elephant Headed for the Swamp

The fall term of school had let out for Christmas. The weather had been cold, for an East Texas winter, with norther after norther battering the woods. But the week before Christmas Day went all fair and balmy, the way it can often do down in the Big Thicket country.

Will Henry had met Chuck on the porch of the store, where Uncle Sol was enjoying a brief respite from the confines of the space behind the heater. In a bit Tim and his brothers joined them, and they all indulged in a strawberry pop.

Sol leaned his chair back against the wall and sighed. "I know you boys are wishin' for Christmas to come, but I'm looking a long way past that, to spring. My old bones are goin' to shout Hallelujah when the weather warms up to stay. Makes me think of the old days, when I was your age and didn't really know what a pain was—not a real, bone-cracking, come-to-set-up-housekeeping-and-stay pain, that is. I used to wish for the circus to come to Tompkins the way you all are wishing for next Thursday to come. We never had much Christmas, outside of a big feed with all the relatives coming to visit, but the circus—now that was something special." He sighed and tucked his thumbs into his galluses.

Will Henry and his crew seldom saw a circus, and when they did it was one of the small flea-bitten ones that had replaced the great tent-shows of the past. "I don't see anything so special about a circus. Christmas, now—we'll get new bikes, maybe, or a space helmet and ray-gun or something really neat. Circuses just have elephants and such."

"Just have elephants?" Sol looked shocked. "The first elephant you ever see close up is the most awesome thing in the world, boys.

And the elephants when I was a boy were bigger and fiercer and more independent than any they seem to have, nowadays. Why the one that strolled into the swamp was as big as Will Henry's house, mighty near."

"Into the swamp? Our swamp?" Chuck's eyes were round, and his red-rimmed mouth was wide.

"Our swamp. They had a tent show right here in Possum Creek, set up out on the meadow where Hanks's hayfield is now. They had ponies with red bows in their manes and a bunch of camels and a bear and an elephant the size of Kingdom Come. Not to mention girls in little bitty skirts that didn't cover their you-know-what's that rode ponies or camels or swung around on the trapeze.

"They come into Tompkins in trucks, and when they decided to do a one-night show way out here there was some excitement, you'd better believe. Yale and William and me spent the night with our cousin Andrew and was waiting beside the road before daylight, the morning they was due in; they arrived along about nine o'clock. They get up early, those show people." He was grinning with re-membered bliss.

"It's hard to think of a circus coming all the way out here," said Chuck. "Nothing ever comes out here, nowadays."

"Back then, strange as it seems, there was a lot more folks in the county outside the towns. Now, just about everybody lives in town and the farms have growed up in trees and weeds. But then every inch of land was either being farmed for cotton and corn or was growing pine timber. There was a big bunch of folks there the night the circus gave its big show. They had no reason to regret coming so far to do it—every seat in the tent was full, and people stood at the back and in the aisles."

"About the elephant," Les piped up. "How did it get loose?"

"Nobody ever quite figured that out. They packed up everything after the show, but they didn't intend to pull out until daylight. The livestock was penned up, and the elephant was chained to a big iron stake that they drove into the ground up to the ring on its top. But I reckon, when an elephant wants to go for a walk, there's nothing much in the world that can stop it. And about two o'clock in the morning, that sucker pilled up his stake and strolled over to eat Mrs. Thrash's pet rosebushes, under her bedroom window. She come alive, I'll tell you!"

Solomon began to chuckle, sending waves of fat rolling over his rotund shape. "I was spending that night in Possum Creek with my cousin Andy, too, on account of going to the circus, and we heard something that sounded like Gabriel's trumpet. Woke us right up.

By that time, menfolks was getting their britches on and going out to find out what was happening. Mrs. Thrash's son was out in their yard with his shotgun in both hands, but he hadn't fired a shot.

"'Where do you shoot an elephant?' he was asking everybody who got there. 'He was big as the house, and I aimed at his side, but it looked useless to hit him there. Then I aimed at his leg, but that would leave him three more, while I reloaded, and I didn't relish being squashed by any dad-blamed elephant.'"

Will Henry was holding his pop bottle in both hands, squeezing it in the middle in his excitement. An elephant on the loose, eating rosebushes and facing down men with shotguns was a far cry from the patient and tired animals he was used to seeing on TV when they had a circus on.

"Well, by that time, that elephant decided he wanted to see the woods and the swamp, and he just strolled on down through Thrash's cornfield to the creek and ambled down that until he hit the trees. Then he thought he was in elephant heaven.

"He'd reach up and gather in big swatches of leafy branches and tuck 'em into his mouth. Then he'd stroll on a little farther and do it all over again. When he came to the humongous tall tupelo gum that used to stand above everything else, he just put his head against it and shoved until the thing come down with a crash.

"Well, you'd better believe that the Mighty Elephant Hunters were being careful. By then the circus folks was there, and of course they didn't want their beast damaged. Besides which, they said that anything short of a big-bore elephant gun wouldn't do a thing but upset that critter and make him mad. So a lot of the men slipped back home and put away their .22 rifles and their twelve-gauge shotguns.

"Then we just followed along, watching what that animal did. He ate up the tops of about a dozen trees before he figured he was full. Then he set off for the swamp, as if he smelled freedom down there and was ready to go for it.

"There was a big round moon out, that night, and you could see most as good as day. The elephant—if I recall right his name was Sultan or something like that—set off down the wagon road that used to go to the old boat landing, right near where you boys caught that great big bass, last summer. The dust was pale like powder, and we could see little puffs rise up when he picked up his big round feet.

"All of a sudden, Sultan gave a gosh-awful squeal through his trunk and stopped dead in his tracks. His ears went up, and I never saw anything look as scared as that critter did."

"What could scare an elephant?" asked Chuck in a choked voice. "Must have been somethin' terrible."

"I guess it was, to Sultan. His keeper went out into the track and called to him, and he wheeled around, those big ears flappin', and came running like a baby to its mama. The keeper put a hook sort of thing up around his ear and drug himself up onto his back and rode him off back to the circus.

"And we went out in the road and looked to see what in the world could have turned that monster into a mess of jelly. And it was a possum. Just a little old skinny-tailed possum, going about his business in the middle of the night, like possums was made to do."

The boys looked at each other, disgust in their eyes. Sol nodded again. "The circus people told us that elephants is scared stiff of a mouse, and I guess that possum looked to it like the hugest mouse in Creation. Anyway, what a whole town full of men with guns couldn't manage to do, one little old possum did without even intending to. The next morning the circus people paid Mrs. Thrash for the damage to her rosebushes and pulled out before Sultan took it into his head to ramble around any more in Possum Creek."

Chuck sighed and finished his pop. "I guess I'll look closer at the elephants, when they come on TV," he said. "Seems as if nothing is as good or as big or as mean as it used to be, though. Even elephants."

Solomon Peat grunted and leaned his chair back against the wall. "Well, I'll tell you, Chuck, that things seem to shrink as time goes past. Nothing I recall from when I was your age is as big or as fine or as impressive as I used to think it was. I 'spect you'll find that true, as you get older, too. There's something about getting older that just takes the steam out of things. But it's always good to recollect how they were, anyway, don't you think?"

The boys nodded as they put their pop bottles carefully into the case and hopped off the porch. It was the wrong time of the year to try to catch catfish, but a big "imaginary elephant" hunt sounded like something that even the winter woods might embellish.

XXIII.

MOLLY MILKED THE GOAT

One of the brief and spring-like spells was lighting the winter woods with sun and making even the birds tentatively try out their spring calls. Uncle Sol, in his usual chair on the porch of the store, was talking a blue streak to the wide-eyed boys when his spate was suddenly shut off.

A brown-haired girl came zooming down the road on a bicycle whose front tire kept getting into the leftover ruts from the week before and almost pitching her over the handlebars. She wobbled badly a time or two, but she made it to the store and leaned the battered machine against one of the posts.

"'Lo, Sol," she grunted, as she climbed the steps and went inside.

Solomon Peat looked after her, and Will Henry, much to his amazement, saw nothing but admiration in the china-blue eyes. "Who's that, Uncle Sol?" he asked. "I never saw her around here before, and I thought I knew ever'body in Possum Creek. She looks like somebody you wouldn't cross, to me."

Sol sighed and spat. "You are one hundred percent dead certain right about that," he said. "That's Molly Wexham, old lady Tilley's granddaughter. She's been here about a week, since Miz Tilley had that stroke. I recall when that one was just a tad. Most determined child ever growed up in Cotton County, or I'm a whip snake."

Will Henry thought about that for a moment. The girl was lean and still browned from the summer. Her jeans were faded with work, not chemicals, and her T-shirt had a dragon on it, with DON'T BREATHE ON ME! lettered under the faded colors of the picture. She wasn't the sort of a girl he had seen much of, because Cotton County girls had been a little slow about taking up new ways of doing things.

"What makes you say that?" he asked, knowing that those were the magic words to Uncle Sol. He settled against the porch post to listen to whatever tale might come, now.

But Solomon was gazing off over the pine tops, as if he was traveling back in time. It took a poke at his knee to bring him back to the present.

"What makes you say that? About Molly What's-her-name?" Will Henry asked again.

"Wait till she's gone!" the old man mouthed at him, wordlessly.

Sure enough, the quick tread was coming toward them from the store, and Molly herself bounced across the porch, holding a brown paper bag on her hip, and hopped onto the bicycle. She rode one-handed (sometimes no-handed, Will Henry noticed with admiration) and scooted back up the road, ignoring the sashays caused by the ruts.

Sol sighed audibly. "That girl has more guts and git-up than a whole passel of what used to pass for 'ladies' 'round here," he said. "Her Ma died when she was tiny, and her Pa brought her back here to his wife's mother, Miz Tilley. Then he went and got hisself killed over in one of them Ayrab countries, and there she was with the old lady, just the two of 'em by theirselves.

"Miz Tilley had a little pension from her dead husband, and Molly had some insurance from her Pa, so they got along pretty good, but they gardened and raised rabbits and chickens. Only thing they didn't have was milk—Miz Tilley thought this bottled milk that's been heated up and cooled down and done this-an-that-to was fit to kill a young'un of hers, so she wanted fresh, strained, guaranteed real milk. She bought them a goat."

Chuck, leaning against the other side of Will Henry's post, sat up suddenly. "My Aunt Lee got a goat, once," he said. "It butted Uncle Samuel over the hood of his car, when he bent over to polish it in the middle. He sent it to the locker plant and had it made up into barbecue."

"They're ornery critters," said Sol. "As Molly and her grandma found out right from the start. They named that nanny-goat Elsie, and Elsie took and chased Miz Tilley around the house four times before she could get ahold of the door handle enough to let herself inside. When Molly saw what was happening, she went in the kitchen and got her a nice strong stick of kindling wood. She wasn't more'n nine years old, if that, but even then she was as hard-headed as a cypress stump." He began to chuckle, sending ripples of fat down his rotund belly.

"That little old young'un headed after that goat, and then the shoe was on the other foot, Miz Tilley told me. Chased old Elsie round and round till she tried to go through the garden fence. That caught her long enough for Molly to catch up, and then she dragged that goat by the ears to the porch and yelled for her gramma to bring her an old stocking. Well, Miz Tilley rummaged around and found an old black silk stocking that she'd been keeping to strain lye soap through, and she took it out on the porch.

"Molly tied that goat hand and foot, if it can be said that a goat has a hand to tie. Looped the stocking around her right back leg and up around the porch post and pulled it up so's Elsie couldn't kick or get her foot in the bucket. The front end of Elsie was dancing a jig, but the back end stayed still while that kid milked her, right there beside the porch.

"That seemed to sort of break her spirit. She never chased people again, and when it come milking time she stood just as pretty, though Molly always tied up that leg. She didn't trust Elsie as far as she could toss a bear."

Will Henry leaned forward, trying to see if the bicycle and its rider were still in sight. But only a thin wisp of dust showed where they had passed.

"When she was only nine years old?" he asked.

"Just about. Not bigger'n a cricket. She milked that goat until she went away to college. Got her a scholarship and went for four years and then she went to work for this here Nasty place that put the men up there on the moon. Says she's going herself, when she can talk 'em into it."

The boys' eyes were wide, thinking of it. They remembered seeing films of that amazing trip to the moon, though none of them were big enough to remember it. Will Henry's mother had told him he watched it, but to his disgust he couldn't recall a thing about it.

"And that lady is going to the moon?" The thought boggled his mind. He hadn't a doubt of it—she'd go. Anybody that could tie up a goat with a silk stocking and milk it, at the age of nine, was going to do anything she put her mind to, that was plain as paint.

"She'll go," said Sol, his voice very soft and sure. "Oh, you can bet your last pair of galluses on it. Molly Wexham will go to the moon."

The boys drank the last of their almost-forgotten strawberry pop, thinking hard about that. Then, without speaking, they nodded their thanks to Uncle Sol and wandered up the road, watching those precious bicycle tracks as if they might lead to some strange and exotic place where none of them had ever gone before.

XXIV.

A BLACK DOG IN THE SNOW

January had blown in on a blue norther that froze the fine rain onto the trees and grass and dripped long icicles off the porch at Mrs. Bragg's store. The ground froze until it crackled, and the snow that came down the next evening frosted everything over with a coat of crystals.

The road was calf-deep, for this was a dry snow, very unlike the sort that seemed to fall in East Texas about every five or six years. Usually it was damp and heavy and compacted beautifully into snowballs and snowmen. This was useless for such things, for it fell apart at once.

Will Henry, bundled to the eyes in jacket and scarf and long underwear and plush-lined gloves and knitted cap, stumped down the way, feeling that he could probably roll as easily as walk. His mother had put two flannel shirts on him, on top of the long-Johns, and then a sweater under the jacket that topped off the mess. He was as wide as he was tall, it seemed, and he could hardly move.

His nose was like a lump of ice, and when he took a breath it burned and froze right down through his lungs. A cold day in the swamp country, with the humidity standing at fifty percent, goes right through to the bones, he was thinking, as he plowed forward, one snow-laden boot at a time.

The tin roof of the store was steaming gently, with damp plops of snow dropping onto the stiff bushes around the sides. The stove would be red-hot, and Uncle Sol would be sitting behind it with his Liar's Award mug in his hands, a story ready, as usual.

But when Will Henry clumped up the slippery steps and stamped his boots to remove the snow, Mrs. Bragg put her head out and said, "Might as well save yourself the trouble. Sol's sick, this morning. His neighbor just came in and told me. He'll be laid up for a while—put his back out when he got out of bed, this morning."

The thought of Uncle Sol being out of commission was one that had never crossed the boy's mind. Sol was as permanent and unvarying as the pines or the swamp or the river itself. A feeling of uneasiness filled him as he thanked the storekeeper and turned his steps back to the road.

Will Henry did not, however, go homeward. He passed the side-road leading to his home and kept going toward the one leading to Uncle Sol's house. He had to see for himself that nothing worse than a bad back was keeping his friend abed.

Uncle Sol lived in the biggest, fanciest house in Possum Creek. Anyone meeting him at Mrs. Bragg's for the first time might be tempted to offer him charity, for he dressed in comfortable overalls, loose cotton shirt, and he stuck his feet into the oldest, softest shoes he could find, ignoring socks except in winter.

However, Solomon Peat, as Will Henry well knew, had begun working in the lumber mill in Tompkins as a young man and had progressed to supervisor. At that point, he had begun taking courses at the nearby college, taken a degree, then another, and before he was ready to retire he had started his own plywood plant and spent years on the faculty of the college's business department.

So the house he had built for his wife, now years dead, was made of the finest woods by the best carpenters available, in an era when carpentry was a fine art. The veranda across the front was now frosted with snow and icicles, but the windows were steamy, and a cheerful light streamed out into the gray day from upstairs.

Willa Reed, Sol's cousin who kept house for him, opened the door, when he tapped. "Gracious, child, come in here before you freeze your tail off!" she said, tugging him into the wide hallway and helping to unwrap him from his layers of clothing.

Will Henry had met her only a few times, for ordinarily he talked with Sol at the store. But he liked her a lot: she was a feminine version of Solomon Peat, less hefty but equally blue-eyed and talkative.

"Solomon will be so glad to see somebody—he was griping this morning about having to stay in bed, when he really had counted on being down at the store to talk to folks about the snow. It's been a long time since we had one when the ground was cold enough to hold it." She hung the last scarf on the hall tree and shooed him toward the stairway. "You go on and cheer him up. He needs it."

Will Henry had always loved his kinsman's stair. It curved up into a branching landing, with a white railing around the edges. The door facing the stair opened when he tapped on it, and a husky voice said, "Willa, I told you I don't need rubbing or baking with a heat-lamp or any other such nonsense. What I need is a new back!" The tone was not Sol's usual cheery one.

"Uncle Sol? It's Will Henry. I went to the store, but Mrs. Bragg said you had hurt your back, so I came on over to see how you're getting on."

There came a groan and a heaving of the brown and orange coverlet that was mounded on the four-poster. Uncle Sol's tousled fringe of hair framed his surprised expression. He struggled to push himself higher on the pillows behind him, wrinkling his forehead ferociously against the pain of moving.

"I tell you boy, don't ever get old. It's for the birds!" he grunted, settling himself with the coverlet pulled under his chin. "Come here and set in Willa's rocker and tell me what it looks like outside. I can see from the window that the snow is looking like one of them frosted Christmas cards."

"That's just about it. And it's cold as blue blazes, too. I saw Hatchett's big black dog trying to cross the creek, this morning, and he went skating everywhichaways, like the cows you chased that time when you were a boy."

Sol's eyes took on a brighter gleam. He heaved a sigh and began looking off past Will Henry into the olden days, and the boy knew that a story was on its way.

"I know that dog well. He reminds me of old Whiz, my English setter that Millie gave me for our first Christmas together. That was the darndest dog you ever saw in your life. Quiet as anything, most of the time. Hated cats and chickens, which was why I kept him penned when we weren't hunting or off running him to get him in condition for the fall and bird hunting. That dog had the judgment of a man. By gum, it was better than a man's, sometimes. I'll never forget...."

"What?" Will Henry was sitting forward, his eyes round, waiting for the story. "You'll never forget what, Uncle Sol?"

"One November afternoon, not too different from today. Winter come early that year, and we had a freeze and then a big snow, and I was too young to have bat sense, so I went off hunting with my brother William, that you was named for. We froze our toes and our noses and scared up some birds, though they had better sense than we did and was settled nice and snug in a brier patch.

"Well, we flushed 'em, after Whiz pointed, and I got two and William got one, and we went on and went on, getting colder all the time, until we decided that enough was enough. The sun was behind clouds, like it had been all day long, and it was about to get dark by three o'clock. So we staggered back to the car and called in Whiz, who was glad enough to come.

"I dropped William off at his house, and he asked me in, but I was all damp and snowy and wanted a cup of coffee the worst way. Will didn't keep coffee in the house, because it made him drunk as a coot, and I intended to stop at the coffee shop that used to be in Possum Creek, over by the cotton gin.

"Whiz was glad enough to stay in the car, down on the floor the way I taught him to stay. Never did have a dog I let get up on the seat. Black as he was, and dark as it was getting, he was purely invisible.

"I was drinking my coffee and shooting the breeze with Claud, who ran the shop, and we both was staring out the big window toward my car, watching the last of the light in the west. It had turned the low clouds pinkish—real pretty."

Sol sneezed sharply, which wrenched his back again, and he let out a yip. But once he had himself settled again, he went on.

"One of the fellows that lived down on the river and worked at the gin in season and did field work in season and just bummed around the rest of the time was coming across the road toward the coffee shop. He cut right beside my car, and my shotgun was layin' across the back of the seat.

"Now I'd left the window part-way down, so Whiz wouldn't stink up the inside so bad, and that fellow just stuck his hand in and grabbed the stock of that shotgun, without any pause or hesitation.

"And then he let out a whoop you could hear clean to Tompkins. Something black come shooting up from the floorboards and grabbed him by the arm, and there he stuck, because you didn't pull anything out of Whiz's teeth if he intended to hold on. And he did intend to hold on, which he did until I got out there and told him to let go."

Sol chuckled. "That man come right into the shop and threatened to have the law on me for having a vicious dog that lunged out the window and attacked him. He was bumptious, that one, which is probably why Simon Watterby killed him, a few years later, when he caught him robbing his hardware store at Mills Fork.

"Claud had seen the whole entire thing, of course, and he just leaned over the counter and said, soft and gentle, 'Mr. Clevenger, I saw you put your hand into that car and take hold of Sol's shotgun. And any jury in the county will take my word for that. That dog was doing what a good dog does, and don't you forget it.'

"Of course, he backed down, and before spring he moved his

family away from Possum Creek, and the river was all the better for him not living down there. And Whiz got a dish of chicken dressing when I got home and Millie found out what he'd done. She was always partial to that dog, anyway. I was too, as you may believe.

"I can see him right now, a black dot against all that snow, pointing pretty as a picture till we kicked up that covey of birds...." Solomon sighed again, staring into the past, as he did more and more often, these days.

That made Will Henry uneasy. He hitched himself around on the rocker as Willa stuck her head in the door.

"Anybody here game for cocoa and cookies?" she asked. "It's just the day for that sort of thing."

"You bet," said the boy. He turned to stare at Uncle Sol. "Don't you want some cocoa and cookies?"

"Didn't think you could drink anything but strawberry pop," grumbled the old man, smoothing down the coverlet so the tray that Willa brought in could sit level. He looked much more cheerful than he had before, and his eyes were bright as he accepted his tray.

Will Henry grinned as he helped Miss Willa place the steaming cups on a side table and pass around the plate of chocolate chip cookies. Uncle Sol might not be in his accustomed place, but the stories were still there, on tap for anyone who wanted them.

As long as that was true, there was nothing much wrong with the world.

XXV.

February Thaw

The winter crept past. Sol grumbled and groaned until he was able to make it down to the store again. Then he groaned some more about the no-count people who let a little mud and chilly weather keep them indoors. But, as Mrs. Bragg kept reminding him, there was more than just a little mud in Cotton County.

The incredible snow had been deep. When it began to melt, as January came up with its usual warm spell, rain began to fall, as well. The dirt roads were like red-mud puddings, and the creeks had overrun their banks and covered pastures and fields. Sundown Swamp was a lake, the fat trees standing hip-deep in water.

The river could be heard clear up to the store, growling among the snags and stumps that had come down with the flood from the forests to the northwest. Caz Carpenter, who had raised about fourteen mahogany-colored children on the proceeds of fishing in that river, claimed never to have seen it higher or more vicious.

"Taken my boat right out from under me," he said, turning his back to the stove to let the damp steam out of his mackinaw. "All my nets is gone, clean down to the Cottingham Fork. The set-hooks that I keep out all winter long, most years, may be down there some'ers, but they're tied onto the willow trees six feet under water. I may have Grampa Catfish hooked onto one of 'em, but there's no way to tell."

Solomon sipped hot coffee from his Liar's Award mug and grinned. "I've seen it fuller, Caz, and you have, too. You 'member the spring of nineteen and thirty-four?"

Caz's black eyes widened, leaving a pale rim around the irises. His normal coffee color paled as if someone had poured milk into it. "Lord, Mr. Sol, I hadn't thought of that since I was a boy. Don't go remindin' me about that flood. I been tryin' to forget that ever since it happened."

As usual, Will Henry and Tim were huddled behind the stove, being quiet and making their strawberry pop go as far as possible. Now Will Henry leaned around a stack of cereal boxes and caught Solomon Peat's eye.

"What happened, Uncle Sol?" he asked. "A flood is just a flood. I can remember three or four, just in the past few years."

The old man shook his head. His back problem had taken away his appetite, and he was no longer quite as round, his blue eyes no longer quite as bright as they had been, but the question sparked them up again.

"That there flood of nineteen and thirty-four was the grand-daddy of all floods. It begun the work of cutting the lake back into the river, you'd better believe, and a lot of other stuff, too. Among which was undercutting the bluff and taking out Howserville, lock, stock, and barrel."

"I never heard of no Howserville," Tim said. "Thought I knew every little old town up and down this here river."

Caz turned to steam the other side of his mackinaw. "That's 'cause there ain't no Howserville left, not a scrap, not a stone, not a nail of it. Not a cemetery of it...." He looked at Sol and went silent, for this was Sol's story to tell.

"That's the God's truth," the old man said. "There used to be a high old bluff up above Crawfish Loop, where the shallows are now. That water was twelve foot deep, if it was an inch, and the fishing would have been mighty good, if old man Steve Howser hadn't of picked that spot to start his dinky little old town, back around the turn of the century. They fished it to death, those Howsers, and they dumped their trash in it, and it was a mess and a half. I didn't like but one of them, to tell the truth, but I wouldn't wish what happened onto a yellow dog."

"Well, tell us about it!" Will Henry insisted.

Sol sighed. "They built a bunch of slab houses up there on the bluff, to begin with, my Daddy told me. Then they got busy and cut a bunch of the timber back in the woods behind the river and rebuilt solid frame houses with brick chimneys and big wide porches they could sit on in the evening and watch the river. It was a right pretty town, and the girls—well, the Howser girls were mighty good to look at. I almost married one, instead of Millie."

He spat quietly into his snuff can and stared at the glowing side of the heater. "Mighty pretty girl, she was, though her daddy was a pistol. They lived right near the river edge of the bluff, and the old cemetery that old man Steve had started when they planted him was beside the house. They hadn't a notion, when they began, how big that settlement would get or that it would finally have a road to it and a mayor and all that stuff.

"And there they set, getting richer from selling timber off the four sections of land the old man had bought from the Mexican that had it from the King of Spain. The First World War really set them up. The girls married outsiders, and instead of going away, they all come right there and built more houses, until that whole entire bluff was streets and lawns and houses, and nothing but the cemetery was open space. And it was getting full, for the Howser connections, blood kin or not, never did play it cautious. They got killed in the damndest ways—logging or rafting down the river in floods or playing with water moccasins. They just seemed to think up silly ways to die."

This was a tale worth hearing. Even Mrs. Bragg, who had come there as a bride long after 1934, was leaning on her counter to hear better.

"So there was the river, flowing free down through the woods, until it hit that messed up stretch where the big bend was, right under that bluff. And there came a flood like nothing we've seen since. This isn't even a peediddle, compared to that. Well, when all the logs and stuff that washed away upstream come tumbling down and hit that garbage the Howsers had dumped into the big eddy, they just naturally hung up. Built a sort of dam, we figured out later.

"And there was too much water coming down to put up with any dam. It just put its back into it and began washing away the dirt of that bluff. Understand, now, that this is the way we put it together later. There wasn't nobody left alive to tell us the right of it, but this sounds reasonable, don't it, Caz?"

"It's about the onliest way," the fisherman agreed.

"If I'd married Lucy Howser, instead of Millie Grant, I'd probably have moved up there and wouldn't be setting here tellin' you the tale," Sol said. "For when Howserville come down, it come all at once and together, living and dead all in one mess of mud and blood and shouts and screams, I have no doubt. Cats and dogs, rose gardens and Ford cars and mules and horses and wagons and logging tools, all at once."

"Wow!" said Will Henry, under his breath.

"How'd you find out about it?" asked Mrs. Bragg, who usually didn't lower herself to get involved in Solomon's tales.

"Why, when the bodies began coming down and floating through folks' yards, which wasn't more than half a day after it happened. It was still raining blue murder, and every house that wasn't built up on high ground or on stilts in low country was already floated away down toward the Gulf. Folks had refugeed to the places that was still sound and dry, and whole bunches of families was camping above the flood, waitin' it out. You know the old Murdock place, used to be down near Sundown till they tore it down?"

Mrs. Bragg thought for a moment. "Oh. Yes, it was one of the cypress houses like they used to make before they cut all the cypress out to sell. Must have been ten feet off the ground, way up on stilts, and two-storied, too."

"There was water in its attic. The preacher went down in a boat to see if the Murdocks got out all right, which they did, not being at home at all when the flood hit. He took a picture of that house with nothing but the roof and half of an attic window showing above the water. So you can see why water was clear back up here in Possum Creek, and the store that was here then was washed entirely away."

"Go on about the bodies," whispered Will Henry, tugging at Sol's sleeve.

"Well, you can see how it was that when the stuff that floated away from Howserville got past the steep banks just upriver, it spread out all over Kingdom Come. And I was setting with Caz and his folks in the loft of my Uncle Sim's house—that was your other great-great uncle, Will Henry—when Caz here let out a yell. 'Lord A'Mighty!' he yipped, 'here comes a dead body!'

"We all ran to the loft door and the windows and looked out, and there was a lump, all soggy and mud-colored, but when it rolled over in the current you could see it had been a woman. Her hair was all streamed out on the ripples, and her eyes was wide open, still looking scared to death."

The boys drew together in the single chair they occupied, and a delicious shiver quivered over their combined flannels and woolens.

"Susanne Howser, that was. Uncle Sim's wife knew her. And she was just the first, though not all of 'em made it down, not by a long shot. In a little bit, there come a seat out of an automobile, sashaying along, still with its wool motoring robe tucked around the edges. And by then we understood that something uncommonly nasty had happened upriver.

"I took out in Uncle Sim's big heavy boat that had a real gasoline motor to run it. Caz and me, we headed out toward the river, watching everything that floated, which kept us pretty busy, as you might imagine. And before we got even with the last cornfield, which was maybe twenty feet below us, I saw that coffin."

"Coffin?" The word was breathed by three different people, for

Mrs. Bragg was now caught up in the story to the point at which she was neglecting a customer. Which was fine, for the young man with the sack of flour was listening, too.

"It looked new, not moldy like they got in the days before they put 'em inside vaults. It was shiny black with silver trim and handles, and there was a wreath of white carnations still stuck onto its top, though they was wilted. And I figured, right off, that somebody had been ready to bury, probably with folks setting up with him, when the flood sent 'em all off together. And that was a shivery thought, sure enough."

Caz perched on a barrel of tacks and nodded. "I still don't like to think on them times. Got enough problems with live folks. Can't really get up no enthusiasm for dead ones no more."

"Anyway, we got a rope onto it and pulled it back up to the house. Tied it to the big old hickory tree that's still there in the yard. Then we went off again, and like the young fools we tended to be, back then, we really enjoyed the excitement. I mean, we understood how bad this thing was, but still, it was different and dramatic, and we got a nice thrill out of it.

"Until I found Lucy Howser, floating face up in an eddy. That shook me. I'm the first to admit it. To find a girl you've fancied, canoodled with a little bit, thought about marrying, even, dead and cold and blue is something that shakes you up pretty bad. And she wasn't the last. All in all, we found fifteen of 'em, and Lord knows how many others floated right past and wound up in the Gulf of Mexico. Some of the ones we found was fresh. A lot of 'em was in rotten old coffins that just barely floated along. No telling how many of those just sank with all hands on board." Sol shuddered and took another sip of coffee.

"We had to wait till the water went down, of course. And when that happened, that coffin upended itself, hanging from the hickory, 'cause we forgot about it in all the excitement. Had to straighten out the old fellow inside before he could be buried. But we needed to find out what happened, first.

"There was no way for anybody to get upriver, and that was before they had helicopters like they have now. But as soon as we could get out and tell the sheriff, a bunch of us started out to see if there was anybody left up at Howserville that needed help. It was all volunteers, for as you can figure, the sheriff and his people were almighty busy with the damage all over this county and a bunch of others around us.

"We rode mules. Nowadays, they'd prob'ly get tractors or Jeeps or some such, but there is no way you can stick a good mule, and that was what got us through the woods and over the creeks and back over that washed-out road that led to the town. And when we got there, there was no town there at all, no way.

"Just a big batch of dirt and lumber and rock all tumbled down into that hole in the river until it wasn't a hole any more. Never has been again. Now it's shallows, though the water's been washing past it for over forty years, now. The river just went around it and cut another channel, and it's ignored the place ever since."

"You didn't find anything?" asked Mrs. Bragg, her black eyes bright with curiosity. "Not a bit of a house or a sidewalk or anything?"

"We found a big raw spot, with a road ending at the edge of it. There was one single tombstone leaning out over the water, with no grave beyond it. There was a set of steps, but the house they'd led up to was gone. No, Miz Bragg, there was nothing that would rightly tell you a town had been there at all."

Caz sighed gustily. "Makes me plumb appreciate little bitty old floods like this one, that don't take nobody's house off or drown whole towns full of folks. Now I don't mind so much goin' out there and gettin' all wet and muddy on my way home. See you, Mr. Sol."

He picked up his bag of groceries and nodded to Mrs. Bragg, who folded her credit book and put it back into its box. The door opened, as he left, followed by the fellow with the flour, letting in a damp breeze that chilled off the interior, despite the efforts of the stove.

Feeling that he had done his duty for the day, Sol rose painfully and put on his heavy fatigue jacket that had been his adopted son's. Mrs. Bragg came out from behind the counter and made sure his cap was on so as to keep his hair dry. She might fuss and fume at him, but Sol was not only her best attraction for the store, he was also her very good friend.

As he walked up the sloppy road, the old man found himself remembering, still again, that long-ago flood. It did, indeed, make you appreciate reasonable ones.

XXVI.

A GREAT BIG BOWL OF RICE

February had come, and the tips of willows were touched with green. The sun warmed away the last of the flood waters, and some bold souls were already breaking their garden spots, putting in turnip greens and lettuce and English peas.

The breeze blew warm from the south, and Solomon Peat was once again sitting on the porch of the store, his denim jacket hanging from the back of his hickory splint chair. It was a Saturday, and Will Henry had come after a package of rice for his mother. Now he sat on the edge of the porch, his sweater tied around his waist by the arms, sipping a strawberry pop with gusto.

The bag of rice lay beside him, and Sol reached to touch it with his toe. "Can't abide rice," he said. "Used to eat it pretty often, back when I was your age and a bit more, but since World War II I've took a scunner against it. The very thought of it turns me off."

Will Henry glanced down at the edge of the plastic packet, which was peeping out of the brown paper bag. "It's okay. Mama fixes it with chicken, and it's pretty tasty." He gulped another swallow of red liquid.

Sol leaned his chair back against the wall and closed his eyes. "Takes me back," he said, "to when I was young. Did I ever tell you I got drafted into the Army, way back then?"

Will Henry choked and coughed. "You mean you fought the Japs?" he managed to say, at last.

"No," Sol said, rather sadly. "They got me too late. Oh, I went through basic training. I served a good long time in Kansas. But I never fired a shot in anger. Just got well and truly fed up with rice."

"Why?" That was Mrs. Bragg, who had come out to whisk her broom over the steps. "What's wrong with my rice?"

"Not a thing, Araminta. It's any rice at all that gives me fits. After I got through shoveling out that post I never wanted to see a grain of rice again."

Will Henry set his bottle carefully between his blue-jeaned thighs and looked up at Sol. "Okay, Uncle Sol, tell the whole thing. Don't keep tormenting us with little bits of it."

"Well, I wasn't much of a soldier, I must admit," the old man said. "But I went through all their silly little old games that would make an old-time hunter laugh his head off. I finally got done with it, without having to beat the sergeant to jelly, and they assigned me to guard a little old ammunition depot away off to hell and gone in the middle of Kansas.

"They put four other fellows out there with me, one of 'em a corporal. And we set out there for six months, never seeing anybody from week to week but the supply truck. And then it took in and stormed fit to tear things altogether up. Tornados zoomed over, and every time we thought we was going to die then and there. The roads muddied so you couldn't even walk out. And the trucks didn't come for a solid month. I think to this day that they got busy helping with the people that got hurt and forgot all about us."

Will Henry took an absent sip of his pop. "And you didn't have anything but rice to eat." His tone was disgusted.

"Not altogether. You see, they elected me cook. And we got down to nothing but a hundred pound sack of rice and some coffee. There wasn't a thing to cook in but big kettles that must've held thirty gallons, so I filled one, the first morning, and poured in a ten-pound measure of rice."

Mrs. Bragg had gone into the store again, but there came a muffled whoop of laughter from behind the door. "Men!" she snorted. "Helpless as babies!"

Sol sighed, looking martyred. "You never saw so much rice in your life," he said. "It bubbled up and bubbled up and filled the cook shed and worked its way into the sleeping quarters and out the door. By the time the others came in from checking the dump, there was rice everyplace you looked, and I was shoveling it out as fast as I could, but it was staying ahead of me.

"It took us all day to get enough room in that little shack to get out of the weather, and it was still raining, so there was no staying out in it. We had rice in our ears and our mouths and our noses. Our shoes stuck to the floor, and our pants stuck to our legs, and everything everywhere stunk of rice."

Will Henry grinned around the mouth of his bottle. Mrs. Bragg was still chortling inside the store.

"We finally got living space cleared out again, and our beds cleaned up, though the blankets stayed damp for days. The kitchen didn't clean up near as well, and the stove was gunked up from bottom to top. But I was still the cook, they said, and what was left in that pot we ate. Tasted like hell, too."

The chair legs came back down with a thump to the floor. "And I kept cooking rice for ten solid days. It was just too bad to walk the fourteen miles to the nearest farm, and nobody was about to go out on a test range in the middle of the rain to check on us. By the time the supply truck came rolling in again, we was all practically talkin' Chinese and squintin' slant-eyed at each other.

"So I never want to put another grain of rice into my mouth again, if I starve for it!" He glared at the pines across the road, and a breeze flapped his jacket against the chair as if in applause.

Mrs. Bragg came out onto the porch to check if Will Henry had finished his pop, which he had. "You run along home, now," she said, nodding him on his way. "And you, Sol, come in for a bite. I've got gumbo on the stove—with rice."

She grinned evilly, and Solomon Peat groaned to his feet and followed her into the store.

XXVII.

THE RABBIT

Solomon Peat arrived at the store one March morning to find Will Henry waiting on the porch. He looked droopy—it was a Saturday, and Chuck's family had gone on a weekend trip. Tim and Les and Fain had been drafted into helping plant their mother's garden. The only item of interest on this doleful morning was a huge rabbit the boy had brought from someplace and laid under the edge of the plank decking.

"Hey, Uncle Sol, did you ever see such a whopper in your life?" the boy asked, as the old man stumped up the steps and let himself down into his hickory splint chair with a groan of relief.

"Well, let me see. I didn't get a good look, before. Set him up here so I can judge. I've seen some almighty big rabbits in my day." Sol bent over to examine the limp bundle of fur the boy produced.

"Big, all right. Run over on the road? Looks like there's some broke bones in him. Killed him with one clip, I expect. Cars do that. Not like bull pups...."

Will Henry dropped the rabbit back onto the ground and perched on the step. "Bull pups? What have they got to do with anything?"

Mrs. Bragg came out and glared at Will Henry. He was being a pest instead of a customer, and Sol hastened to dig into his overalls pocket for change for a strawberry pop. He had his audience cornered, and he didn't intend for him to get away.

Once the boy was situated out of the way against the wall, nursing his pop along, the old man hitched his chair back and half shut his blue eyes. "Once, I had a rabbit would make that 'un look like a kitten. Biggest son-of-a-...."

"Solomon!" Mrs. Bragg admonished from inside the store.

"Absolutely the most humongous rabbit that prob'ly was ever born in these parts," Sol amended. "My brother Will and me, we decided we was going to raise rabbits for meat. Breed 'em and sell 'em, too. Our folks thought it might be a good idea, being as it was hard to make ends meet down here then, so we got together and worked for two weeks for Old Man Hanks to earn our first bunny. Cute little dickens, black and white, the size of a baseball, just about.

"Well, with baby rabbits, it ain't too easy to see just what sort they are until it's finally too late. We wanted a doe rabbit, but what we got was the biggest, meanest buck rabbit ever born. But it was too late to do anything about it by the time we knew that, and besides we figured one rabbit like Buck was all any family could put up with."

"Why?" asked the boy, around the neck of his pop bottle.

"Well, we had a couple of big old German shepherd dogs, Hal and Lady. They took up with that little rabbit right off. Bathed him with their big sloppy tongues till he was soaked through, carried him around by the scruff of his neck, just teetotally adopted him, you might say. So he grew up thinking he was a dog. And he grew, and he grew, and by the time he was a year old he stood as big as a terrier, near enough.

"There seemed to be a lot more dogs running loose, back then. There was Uncle Ernest's coon dogs and Al Hackberry's two yard dogs and a few that wandered in from neighbors as far off as the river. That rabbit went right out with his adopted family when all the dogs got together in the morning to make their regular rounds of trash heaps and privies and the nearby woods. In the beginning, the other dogs kind of thought he was breakfast, but Hal and Lady put them straight about that.

"And when Buck was finished growing, by golly the regular crew seemed to think he was nothing but another dog, too. It was just when a strange critter joined the pack that things got lively."

"Did they kill him?" Will Henry was big-eyed, now.

"H...Heck no! Because when Buck got his full growth, he could lick most any dog ever born. One of them newcomers would take a dive at that rabbit, and the rest of the bunch would set around with their tongues hanging out of the sides of their mouths, laughing the way dogs do, while he turned a flip-flop and kicked his attacker addled with them big hind feet of his. And then they'd all run off together, happy as could be."

"That," said Mrs. Bragg, emerging onto the porch with her broom, "sounds like the tallest tale you ever told yet, Sol. A rabbit that could lick a dog—never heard of such a thing."

Sol was gazing up the road with a gleeful expression on his round face. "You ask Lucy French. She used to be Lucy Hackberry, and we've watched it happen, many's the time. You just ask her, 'cause yonder she comes with her son Hugh."

A dusty Chevy was picking its way up the rutted road, and when it stopped in the parking space, a dumpy little woman got out and pulled a shopping basket out of the back seat. Mrs. Bragg went down the steps to meet her.

"Lucy, Sol here has been telling us the silliest story, and he swears you can bear him out. Did he ever have a rabbit that could beat a dog?"

The little woman's face split into a wide grin. "Lord, Sol, it's been fifty years since I thought of that crazy rabbit! Never saw anything like it in my life—I remember the time he licked both our hounds at the same time. Slapped one silly and then turned around and did the same to the other. Oh, yes, Mrs. Bragg, I remember old Buck well. Nobody could ever forget a rabbit like that one!"

Mrs. Bragg looked a bit boggled, but she was a fair woman, and she went into the store to wait on Mrs. French, leaving the field to Solomon Peat.

"Well, that went on for two years, nearabout. Buck was old, for a rabbit, and the dogs from far and near knew him and treated him just as if he'd been born one of them. And then Uncle Ernest's second son bought a bull pup. Registered animal, they told us, expensive as all get-out, which we doubted, 'cause Ernest was as hard-timey as all the rest of us. But it was one of them that smells its own upper lip and could drown standing straight up, because its nose is turned up instead of down. Besides being ugly as home-made sin."

"Tim's uncle had one, you remember?" asked Will Henry. "Big white dog, that looked like he'd eat you alive."

"That very kind. And he come rampagin' into the yard, one morning when the dogs was setting around exchanging the news of the night before. First thing he did was spot Buck, who was just being one of the boys, as usual.

"That animal taken off after Buck and was no end of surprised when the rabbit stood his ground. He was used to rabbits heading for the tall timber, once he set out after 'em, and when Buck just set there, lookin' mean, he hardly knew what to do. And then Buck flipped and the bull pup had a face full of rabbit feet slapping him silly before he could back off.

"Then the shoe was on the other foot, sure enough. Buck got through slapping that dog, and then he took out after him. Last thing we saw of either of 'em was Buck chasing that dog off into the

137

woodlot behind our house."

"The last thing you saw? You mean neither of 'em came back?" Will Henry's voice held a note of awe.

"Not one hair of either animal was ever seen again. Will and me and Lucy in there looked many a long day for some trace, but not one did we find. Uncle Ernest was mighty put out, and his son threatened to have the law on us, till Pa asked him how he'd like for word to get out that his registered prize bulldog was chased clean off by a rabbit.

"That put the quietus to him, and that was that. I figured, and Will agreed, that they prob'ly just naturally ate each other entirely up, like as in that poem of Eugene Field's that you have to learn in school. The Gingham Dog and the Calico Cat, you know."

Will Henry shook his head, and Sol sighed. Not learning poetry was another thing he held against modern educational methods. How were the poor kids going to wear out sleepless nights or dull routines without a head full of verse to keep things interesting? But he said nothing about that. The kids couldn't help being short-changed.

"Anyway, we missed that old rabbit a lot. Never got another one, though we talked about it once. But Pa made us see the light. 'A family that's had one Buck,' he said to us, 'would be plumb dis-satisfied with anything else. And not but one Buck ever happened in the history of the world. You can bet on that'."

Will Henry finished his pop absent-mindedly. Then he put the bottle in the crate and thumped down the steps to the dead rabbit. He took it up tenderly and dug a hole with Mrs. Bragg's sharp-shooter shovel. He mounded the dirt evenly and tamped it down with the back of the spade.

"Maybe somebody did that for old Buck, you think?" he asked Solomon.

"I'd like to think so. Yes, I'd purely like to believe that," the old man replied, staring off over the pines across the road as if he were seeing in his mind's eye that long-dead rabbit in all his warlike glory.

XXVIII.

THE HEN-HOUSE DISASTER

March was halfway along, and gusts of wind still were kicking up a ruckus among the pines across the road from Mrs. Bragg's store. Solomon was feeling spryer than he had for a long time, and he'd talked his cousin Willa into walking down to the crossroads with him, just to enjoy the morning.

Mrs. Bragg was sweeping the porch, her one-sided broom sending a tornado of dust and pine needles flying, as they paused in the parking area and waited for her to finish.

"Willa, it's good to see you," the storekeeper said, setting the broom inside the store and descending the steps to stand with them in the balmy wind.

"Look at those sweet gums! They'll be all bloomed out in no time," she said, and Solomon nodded.

"You get to our age, Willa's and mine, and you wonder, every fall, if you'll live to see another spring. And every time it's worth it, no matter how your old bones ached during the cold weather. But I have to admit, Araminta, that a cup of your coffee would put life back into my legs, right now."

He settled into his chair, and the two women went into the store, chattering like a tree full of blackbirds. After a bit, Willa came out holding two steaming mugs, and Mrs. Bragg followed her with a small rocker from inside the store.

Instead of returning to her early morning chores, Mrs. Bragg came out once again with a stool and another mug of coffee, and the three of them sat quietly on the porch, breathing the pine-scented air and listening to the hawk that was circling high overhead. Their mood was broken suddenly by a high-pitched shriek from the direction of the river. Sol sprang to his feet, staring toward the source of the sound, and the women tensed, ready to cope with some emergency.

Then Sol drew a deep breath and chuckled. "Relax, girls," he said. "That was Tempy Monroe's crazy gal. I finally recognized her voice. Nothing to worry about."

As he settled back into the hickory splint chair that had taken on the contours of his rotund shape, his cousin began to jiggle gently with laughter.

"Now what in tunket is wrong with you, Willa?" he asked.

"Made me think of that time, right after I came to live with you and housekeep, when you went out to break up that setting hen." Willa's round face was scarlet, and tears came to her eyes. She took off her glasses and wiped them with a Kleenex.

"Now, Willa, you're not going to tell...."

"You're not the only storyteller in this family, Solomon Peat. You've made everybody in Possum Creek squirm for years with your tales about them and their folks. Now I've got one on you—and yonder comes Ghost Larry, right now. You've ridden him high wide and handsome for years, now, and maybe he'll have a laugh on you, for a change."

Sol sighed and leaned back in his chair. "If you've got to, you've got to, but recall, girl, that I've known you for a long time, too, and there's tales I could tell...."

But she only shook her head and grinned at him.

Larry Wright stumped up the steps and into the store. After a bit, he came out again, sidling nervously past Solomon. Willa put out a hand and stopped him.

"Larry, you've known Sol here for a long time. Did you ever in all that time hear him raise his voice?" She cocked her head up to look into his face.

Wright stopped in his tracks, frowning. "Can't say as I have. Can't say as anybody at all has, come to think about it."

"Would you believe that I heard him scream like a cougar with his foot in a trap, once upon a time?"

Mrs. Bragg joined them again. "Willa, that's hard to believe."

Sol thumped his chair legs down again. "If the tale's to be told, it's got to be done proper," he said. "Willa, you just set back and let me tell it."

She nodded and took a long sip of her coffee.

"Well, when Willa come to take care of me, after Millie passed on, I decided that I needed something to take my mind off things. I ordered some unusual chickens from one of these here fancy places, where you get all sorts of oddball breeds. There was one that taken my eye—big black bird with a rose-colored comb. Black Rose

Comb was what it was called too, which I thought was right practical.

"I raised the chicks in a brooder, and when they got ready to put out in the pen, they were mighty pretty to see, pecking and scratching in the grass. Turned out to be the most prolific birds you ever did see, too. I had six of the ten hens sitting as soon as they was old enough. Decided that was enough, so when Number Seven got all broody, I decided to shut her up away from her nest and change her mood."

Willa burbled a chuckle into her coffee mug. Her cousin frowned ferociously in her direction, but a twitch of a smile touched his lips.

"Now if you've ever been on intimate terms with a chicken, you know the d...darned things can read your mind. If you intend to catch one, she knows it the minute you set foot in the chicken yard, and it's easier to catch the wind in your coat-tail than to lay hands on that feathered varmint. So when I went into the chicken house to get her, she flew off the nest as soon as I bent to come in the door.

"I chased her half the afternoon, and she and the others had a merry old time teasing me, till I finally had to give up and think of something sneaky to do to get her." He sighed gustily.

"Come dark, I went out back, real quiet, and crept into the chicken yard. Not a feather twitched. I eased the door open and went inside the chicken house, though it was always a tight fit for me, being as it's only about four feet by four, with nests along one wall.

"Naturally, you can't see a black chicken on a dark nest in a chicken house at night, and of course I couldn't take a flashlight, because that would set the whole thing off again. So I eased over, counted to the third nest in the row, and pushed my hand under the chicken that was setting on it.

"I could feel her leg, right there handy, so I grabbed a good hold onto it and pulled." At that point Willa broke into a small shriek of laughter, and Sol cleared his throat.

"The chicken flew off, but that leg stayed in my hand and began to squirm. I'd caught hold of a d...darned chicken snake that had gone sneaking under her to hunt for eggs."

"Well, they're not poisonous," Mrs. Bragg said, her voice quivering slightly.

"No, but I don't really like snakes all that much. In fact, they turn my bones to jelly. And any snake's bite is serious, because they've got crazy germs in their mouths that people aren't immune to. Anyway, I turned around to get outside, still holding the snake because at least that way I knowed where he was, you see. And that little old door seemed like it shrank up to nothing. I could see a patch of stars about the size of my pocket handkerchief.

"That was when I decided I needed some light on the subject, and I started calling for Willa."

Now his cousin was rocking in her chair, her cheeks wet with tears of laughter.

Mrs. Bragg looked shocked. "That wasn't funny, I'd think, standing there in the dark holding onto a snake!"

"The funny thing was that it never dawned on me it might be Sol. I'd never heard him shout in all our lives, and I didn't know he could! I looked out to see if the dogs seemed to smell a cougar, but they just wagged their tails and lay down again.

"I thought maybe Tempy's girl was visiting her kinfolks over across the river, and the water was carrying her cries over to me. It wasn't until the noise just would not stop that I thought to take a flashlight out in back and check on Sol."

"And there I stood, all squinched up in that chicken house, as if it had shrunk around me, holding that four-foot chicken snake. She turned the light on me, and then she had the gall to start laughing. Girl never did have a bit of tact." But Sol was grinning. He appreciated a good story, even if he was the butt of it.

Ghost Larry was grinning, too. "Gonna call you Chicken-Snake Sol from now on," he grunted, as he stumped down the steps and away into the breezy morning.

Mrs. Bragg got up off her stool and put it neatly back into its spot inside the store. She collected the empty mugs and surveyed the porch for pine needles her broom might have missed.

Then she turned to Solomon Peat. "Now that," she said, her tone deep with satisfaction, "is what I call a first-rate story. And be sure that you tell it to those fool children, too, or I'll do it for you. It's time they found out that you're not dead level perfect, Sol." She clumped into the store, and the door closed behind her.

Solomon stared at Willa, who was wiping her eyes. His big round belly began to jiggle, and that set her off again. They laughed together, then, filling the March morning with the sound of their hilarity.

Inside the store, safely out of sight, Mrs. Bragg was smiling broadly, too. And Ghost Larry, well along on his way home, was laughing fit to frighten the squirrels in the budding oak trees.

XXIX.

A SHOT IN THE DARK

Spring had set the blood of young critters to singing. Will Henry felt that every minute he spent in school was directly stolen from really important things that would never come around again.

Besides which, his fishing instincts were beginning to revive. The thought of Grampa Catfish, down there in the river, uncaught and unafraid, kept intruding itself between him and his books. Every time he looked up and caught Chuck's or Tim's eye, he saw that they, too, were about to squirm out of their skins.

But the swamp was too wet to tackle, by far. The floods of early in the year had left the river very high, and much of the low area was still under water. The time to catch Grampa was when water was low and he was trapped in the channel.

The boy sighed and went back to reading his Social Studies book. He would never live until Saturday. He knew it with every drop of blood in his body.

He did, of course. Saturday, however, was chilly, which just went to prove what he had always suspected—there wasn't a bit of justice in the entire world. Uncle Sol was on the porch of the store, however, and that made up for a lot.

Tim and his brothers were coming from the other direction, as Will Henry and Chuck climbed the steps. Sol grinned at his favorite audience and began shelling out quarters. He hated school as much as the boys did, for it deprived him of appreciative ears, and if a few dollars worth of strawberry pop would buy them some time on the porch, it was more than worth it.

As he waited for the five to come back out of the store, he heard a distinctive sound, coming from the direction of Tompkins. His blue eyes brightened, and he sat straighter in his chair as a long black car, patterned with dust from the road, slid to a stop beside the store.

The door opened, and a skinny man slid from beneath the wheel, his lanky frame seeming to take a very long time to untangle its length from the interior of the Cadillac. He completed the task, at last, and reached in to grab a wide-brimmed hat, which he set on his narrow skull with a satisfied thump. When he looked up and saw Sol, he smiled, his pale eyes narrowing and sending smile wrinkles down his cheeks and up to his hairline.

"Well, Pete! Been a while since I saw you," said Sol, rising painfully from his chair and taking the offered hand, as soon as the newcomer reached the porch. "Do most of your trading up in Tompkins, now, I expect. How does Amy like living in the big city?"

"It's all right, but there isn't much excitement," said Pete, shifting a chew of tobacco from his left cheek to his right. "No cougars screaming in the night. No bobcats in the henhouse. No water moccasins in my boots out on the porch. They think such things as robberies and knifings are exciting, poor things, but we know better, don't we, Sol?"

Solomon Peat grinned widely. "Pete McKittridge, you can rustle up more excitement by yourself than the entire town of Tompkins all together, when you put your mind to it."

Pete pushed his hat back, his eyebrows rising. "There have been some crazy things happen, while I lived out in the woods. You recall the bear that tore into my smokehouse and took off a whole winter's pork? That hunt saw more drunks fall into more sinkyholes than any single thing I ever did see.

"Tom Pendleton went home, and his wife wouldn't let him in the house...she didn't recognize him for the mud! And Skunk-Foot Henry got lost and wasn't found for a solid week. Still drunk, as I recall."

Sol was joggling, as he sat in his chair again. "You recall the time you got fed up with the kids using your woods for a lover's lane?"

Will Henry had been listening avidly through the thin wall of the store, as the old cronies talked. But now he shook his head. Mrs. Bragg caught his eye and jerked her head, moving the boys out briskly.

As they dropped to sit on the edge of the porch, McKittridge pulled the other splint chair from its spot against the wall and straddled it, facing Sol. "By gum, it's really good to remember the old days. That hickory woods was full of cars, most Saturday nights, and I wouldn't have cared a lick, if the blame kids hadn't kept leaving my gate open."

144

"They're bad about that," said Sol. "These boys here, once they get a bit of growth on 'em and begin tagging after the girls, they'll lose all their common sense. Won't know better than to leave gates open, so cows will get out on the highway and get hit and cause wrecks."

"Will not!" said Will Henry, around the neck of his pop bottle.

"You just wait," said Pete. He stared at the wall, but it was plain he was looking into the past, the way Sol so often did. "I did, myself, and so did Sol, here. Went plumb silly, we did, for a while. But those cows—that was something entirely un-ac-cep-table."

Solomon laughed. "I never saw anything like those woods in my life, the morning after...."

"You may be the storyteller, Solomon Peat, but this is my tale. Let me tell it, for once," the skinny man said.

"Go ahead," Sol agreed, leaning his chair back against the wall. "I'll put in anything you forget." His eyes twinkled.

"Well, the young folks had used my woods for years. Before they had so many cars to canoodle in, it was all right. Buggies just naturally are more leisurely, and you got out and opened the gate. Your girl drove the animal through, and you shut it and climbed back in. No sweat.

"Cars are different, though. Seems like the young sports couldn't be bothered to get in and out twice. So I lost seven head of Herefords one year, besides gettin' sued for a wreck my bull caused when somebody swerved to miss hitting him. I knew I had to do something to keep them out of the lane. And I found just the ticket, too."

Will Henry had not really cared about hearing a lot of nonsense about teenagers smooching, but this sounded promising. He pricked up his ears. "What did you do, Mr. McKittridge? Lock the gate with a chain?"

"Oh, I'd tried that a good way back. They knocked off the locks or uprooted the post or just plain broke the gate to flinders. No, I came up with something a lot more exciting than that." He grinned reminiscently.

"One Saturday evening, I left the gate wide open and penned all the cattle on the back thirty. Cars went up that lane for an hour and a half, right around dark, and I set still and let things get quiet and interestin'.

"About nine o'clock, I crept out of the house with my double-barreled twelve-gauge and sneaked into the woods. There was a half-moon, that night, and I could see glints of car roofs shining all out through the hickories.

"I took careful aim at the top of the biggest hickory tree there and let off both barrels, one after the other. Sounded like the Trump of Doom, let me tell you! And then stuff came rattling down on the cars, and engines cranked, lights came on, there were yells and screams and cusses and everything else you can think of."

Solomon was chuckling, his belly vibrating.

"There was a real traffic jam, what with all those cars, parked everywhichaway, trying to get out at once. I listened for a while, and then I went home to bed.

"The next morning I met Sol on his way in to town, and I invited him to look over the timber with me. We found the damndest things! There was a pair of shoes with the socks inside, just as if the fellow had jumped straight up out of them. We found panties and shorts and neckties and girdles and wallets and watches and blankets...." He paused for breath.

"Don't forget them stockings that was still hooked onto the garter belt," put in Sol. "I never did figure that one. How a human being got into that contraption I don't know, but how one got out of it all in one leap...well, it just boggles the mind."

"Solomon, you're putting evil ideas into these youngsters' minds." That was Mrs. Bragg, talking from inside the store. "You just get your minds out of the gutter this instant!"

McKittridge looked over at Will Henry and winked. Sol looked smug.

"She's a woman, and they just don't understand male people at all," he whispered. Then, louder, he said, "Well, anyway, Pete, you broke up the lover's lane business for good and all. Never had another cow get out, did you?"

"Not till the tornado took off a mile of fence line," returned McKittridge, rising and setting his chair neatly back into position. "And that was an act of God."

He turned into the store. "Got to get me a dill pickle," he said. "There's not a pickle anyplace that tastes like Mrs. Bragg's, that she keeps in that gallon jar on the counter. While Amy checks out the trunks in the attic at the old place, I decided just to come and get me one for old time's sake."

He grinned slyly at Sol. "Makes me homesick, talking about the old days. But heck, maybe I can think of something that will put some liveliness into Tompkins. You ought to come over and help me think, Sol, one day when you haven't anything better to do."

"Lord help us if the two of you get together to plan mischief," said Mrs. Bragg, coming out of the store with a pickle skewered on a fork. "Here, stop your gob with that!"

Pete took the pickle and bit off a chunk. Then, chewing happily, he turned back to his fancy car and left in a drift of sandy dust.

It suddenly occurred to Will Henry that growing up might not be entirely without interest. Maybe...but he discarded the notion at once. It would involve getting close to a girl, and that was something he knew that he would never, never do.

XXX.

Spring Is a Kind of Madness

The mockingbirds were having a conniption fit in the top of Mrs. Bragg's chinaberry tree. The lemon and white tomcat that lived down the road had decided on baby mockingbird for breakfast, and the frantic parents were swooping in dive-bombing formation, taking tufts of fur from the top of his head with every kamikaze attack.

Solomon, enjoying the warm sun on his arthritic legs, was having more fun than the tomcat was. The animal tried backing down the tree, and the birds attacked from the rear, denuding part of his tail with every dart.

He was beginning to look a bit moth-eaten by the time Will Henry and his crew came charging up the dusty road, their popguns in hand. A few well-aimed chinaberries sent the mockingbirds sailing back to their nest, scolding at the tops of their lungs, and allowed the defeated tomcat to beat a hasty retreat into the shelter of the honeysuckle hedge at the back of the store property.

"He brought that onto himself," Sol objected, as the boys lined up, waiting for their handout. The change jingled in the old man's pocket, as he pulled out the quarters and distributed them into the grimy palms the five held out to him.

Will Henry grinned wickedly. "Be an awful world if we all got what we deserved, Uncle Sol." Leaving his great-uncle to mull over that, he led his bunch into the store, where Mrs. Bragg was already pulling the dripping bottles from the icy water in the cold drink machine.

Once they were back on the porch, Sol seemed uninterested in starting a story, which was highly unusual.

"You sick, Uncle Sol?" asked Will Henry. "You're awful quiet."

He sighed, his faded eyes staring over the pine trees toward the river and the swamp. "I was just recollecting how fine it used to be, fishing down there in this kind of spring weather. Seemed like the worms just crawled up out of the dirt to be found and the fish jumped out of the water after them, once we baited our hooks.

"I'd sit on the bank in the shade, watching my bobber—and it was a dry willow twig, not one of these bought red and white ones— while the minnows made dashes at it. There'd be little bitty crawfish moving around right next to the edge of the water, and perch would come shooting in and upset 'em from time to time. Dragonflies would take a rest on my pole, their wings shiny and nervous in the sunlight.

"The wind would rustle in the new leaves, and every now and then a squirrel would throw down a rotten nut left from his winter stock, and the world would seem so almighty good you could eat it with a spoon."

Even the boys were caught by the imagery. They knew—who better?—all the things he said. Besides which, they still were bound and determined to catch Grampa Catfish, one way or another.

They sat in the sun, enjoying this short time in spring when it soothed instead of biting, sipping their soda pop and thinking of their plans. They knew, now, that the pit trap would work. That twenty-pound bass still hung in all its stuffed and varnished glory on the wall inside the store. Fishermen had come all the way from Tompkins to see it and to try their luck on the river.

It was Saturday. School would be out in three weeks, but already the river had gone back to its normal size, and the swamp had dried enough to allow fishermen and hunters into its depths. What better time, lacking a story, would there be to begin their quest?

"I guess we'll go down and look at the river. Maybe wet a hook," Will Henry said, as the old man showed no sign of talkativeness.

He grunted, shook himself, and stared down at the boys, almost as if he wondered who they were. "I guess I'm lost in the past, boys," he said. "You go on and fish. If there was ever a day made just for that, this is it. Good luck!"

The five filed off the porch and set off down the dusty track toward the river. Every one of them had a fishing line rolled around a stick bobber, the hook firmly embedded so as to spare any boy-flesh coming into range, stuck into his hip pocket.

They had more equipment stashed near the river. They had taken the opportunity, every time the weather permitted, to carry down old shovels and sections of net found along the river after the flood and stout scraps of wood left over from building projects all over Possum Creek. This time they would have a trap that could hold even a three hundred-pound catfish.

There were a lot of people along the river. Old and young, black and white and tan, male and female, they seemed to have the same impulse to put a hook in the water on that tempting spring day.

The boys cut off into the swamp to avoid notice, for among all those warm bodies there had to be some who would know that they weren't supposed to be too near the morass. They had decided on a new spot that had been formed by the flood waters: A different outflow from the swamp had been cut through a sand bar, hidden by thick growths of willow that was tied together with grapevines and sawvines and blackberry vines until they made a wall that hardly a muskrat could wiggle through.

It was mid-morning by the time they were in place. They had detoured past the shed where the great alligator presided, for it had offered a perfect shelter for their accumulation of tools and materials. Three loads apiece succeeded in gathering the stuff at its appointed place.

The water smelled rich—a mix of waterweed, fish, mud, and something indefinable all mingled together. The coffee-colored depths were clear in the shallows, and they could see minnows with white dots in the middles of their heads bustling about, while water bugs skated dizzily over the surface above them. It was a temptation just to lie flat and watch the teeming life in the water and on the mud flats on the other side of it.

Will Henry, however, was a stern taskmaster. He bullyragged the boys into taking turns with shovels and pick. The sun became an enemy, rather than a friend, very quickly, as they toiled and sweated and went down through the soft soil that held only gravel layers, from time to time, to make it harder to dig.

By noon they were six feet down. Every one of them had a pocketful of sandwiches, now squashed flat but still tasty, and Tim came back from a trip to the bushes with wild excitement on his face.

"We kin have milk with our dinner! They's a nanny goat over here that's just bustin' with milk. Must have lost her kid. We kin milk her into the worm bucket!"

Will Henry knew quite a bit about milking, for his folks used to have a cow. He had done some milking under heavy protest, from time to time, and he had also watched the way his mother handled the milk, once it was removed from the cow. That had impressed him a lot.

150

"Anybody got a handkerchief?" he asked, looking from face to face. "Can't drink milk without it's been strained, Mama says. It's not sanitary. No use takin' the trouble to milk her, if we can't use the milk, once it's done."

There came a great searching of pockets. One by one, they shrugged. But Les drew from his overalls a grimy scrap, obviously used for some time without washing.

"I got one!" he said, his round face alight. "We kin go catch that goat right now!"

That was more easily said than done, but the goat being penned in on a sort of island helped a lot. They managed to hem it on the very end, and it showed no desire to go into the water. Will Henry grabbed it by the ears, and Chuck grabbed it around the body.

Then came the time for serious action. Milking a goat that persistently hops up and down on both hind feet can be a strangely unproductive activity. The worm bucket (which had been sloshed in the river a couple of times to sanitize it) was kicked over more than once, before they realized that each of the smallest boys must hold onto one hind leg, while Tim and Chuck held her in place.

That was the solution. Will Henry stretched the handkerchief over the top of the rusty syrup bucket and began squirting streams of milk. Having only two spigots was a little strange, but the milk came far more easily than it does from a cow, so it balanced out.

He filled the bucket almost to the top, and while the result resembled chocolate milk more than the usual kind, none of them had ever seen goat milk before, and they decided that must be its natural color. Still warm from the goat, it washed down the squashed sandwiches beautifully, though the flavor left a bit to be desired.

Refreshed, they took a short nap in the shade of the willows and woke to new efforts. The pit was finished and the shoring boards in place before the sun was too low.

Sunday afternoons were free—that was one of the rules of Possum Creek. If the boys sat still in church and didn't put gum in the hair of anyone in front of them, behaved at lunch, and didn't attract any unfavorable attention, they could go where they would all afternoon.

If the three families involved had compared notes, they might have suspected something. Fortunately they didn't go to the same churches, so that was not a problem.

The five met in the woods and cut straight to the river. There was something odd about their smell, aside from the fact that they were all wearing the oldest, dirtiest things they owned, for each had picked up something dead. A chicken from Chuck's neighbor's yard, a snake that had been run over in the road, a cat that had lost its ninth and last life in the teeth of a Doberman ranging the woods: bait—all bait—to catch that giant catfish.

There was a faint overcast, that afternoon, after a sunny morning. The swamp was swept with shadow from clouds that flew over, from time to time, and there was the feel of rain off in the distance. The boys hurried to bait their trap and take their places, watching until their eyes burned from the glare of light on water.

The afternoon passed so slowly that they felt they had been waiting there for years. The river gurgled behind them and beyond the willows with such insistency that they had to take turns going into the bushes to pee.

Will Henry was beginning to have grave doubts about the feasibility of their plan, when Tim, beside him, gasped and grabbed at his arm. "Look!" He pointed.

A shadow that seemed as large as that of one of the clouds had slid into the runnel. The head, surely as wide as the church sofa if not wider, seemed to be questing, turning this way and that, its feelers (almost like snakes, those were) rippling in the water as it felt/smelled/searched its way toward the pit and its odorous bait.

Will Henry held his breath and touched Chuck, who reached to alert the smaller boys. The five lay on the warm sand, watching, feeling their hearts pound almost to bursting as the huge shape thrust its head into their trap.

They had kept that church sofa in mind, as they dug. The opening was big enough, and more, to accommodate the bulk of the creature. It slid into the slot like a ship into a dock, and the chicken disappeared in one gulp.

Then the boys were frantically busy, lowering their gate, securing its fastenings, and praying to gods that the parents of small boys forget exist. The chicken disposed of, the catfish turned its attention to the dead cat.

"I thought that'd be good," said Tim, with deep satisfaction. "Stands to reason a cat fish would like a cat."

There came a deep chuckle behind them, and Will Henry almost wet his pants. He whirled with the others, to find Solomon Peat standing behind them, his bulk sinking him slightly into the loose sand of the spit.

"You know, I had a notion you fellows were up to something really big. I been a boy myself, recollect, and I recognize the look. Yesterday you all went off too easy. Ordinarily, you'd have pestered me till I told you a tale, but you gave up too quick.

"I got to thinking what I'd be doin', if I was your ages and full of beans like the bunch of you all." He chuckled again, his tone wicked.

"There was just one thing. I put together all the questions you been askin' me for almost a year. I thought about the sounds we been hearin' from the river, since Grampa got loose from the lake, and I made a wild guess. Hit it right on the button, didn't I?"

Will Henry nodded. If this had been another adult, of all those he knew, he might have been frightened or upset or wary, but this was Uncle Sol. He had been in scrapes, himself, and he'd broken most of the rules ever invented.

"We got him, Uncle Sol. Right down here. Look!"

The boys stepped aside to let Solomon stare down into their trap, where the catfish, finding that there wasn't room to turn around, was trying to back out. There was no sign of any of their bait left at all.

"You've got him, sure enough," said Sol. "And now what're you goin' to do with him?"

Will Henry shrugged. "He catches kids," the boy said. "We ought to kill him."

Sol sighed. "I doubt if that fish ever got any of those missing children. The river's been takin' kids for as long as I can remember, and there's gators down here that can dispose of drowned bodies before they can get found. And even if he did get one, now and again, how many of his kind have their folks pulled out of their home and fried in a skillet? Man eats catfish is fine and dandy, but catfish eats Man seems to be mighty upsettin', though it shouldn't. Turn and turn about, boys."

Will Henry had never thought about it that way. It seemed fair, once you thought about it. "He's too big to eat," he said.

Sol nodded. "He'd feed the whole entire county, if he could be et. But he's too old. He'd taste just like river mud, I'd stake my life on it." He looked down at Will Henry, his eyes bright again.

"And what would it be like, Will Henry, to know that he wasn't in the river any more? Never would be again?"

All five boys stared at each other in dismay. They had never thought beyond this point. Life without the big fish—how dull that would be. Almost like life without the river and the swamp and Uncle Sol.

Will Henry looked about at his henchmen. Their eyes met his, and all five nodded. Then, with great deliberation, they began to unfasten the lines and draw up the gate.

XXXI.

Summer and Solomon

School was out. The dust lay thick on the road, and the occasional car or pickup kicked up a tail of pale powder, which settled over the porch and Sol and the boys who sat there sipping strawberry pop.

Something circled, far off over the pine trees, and Will Henry stared after the dot of blackness. After a moment, he turned to look at Solomon Peat. The old man was smiling, rocking his chair gently back on its warped legs.

Mrs. Bragg stumped out and sat down, wiping her forehead on her sleeve. "It's gone and gotten hot, Solomon," she said. "Here, Will Henry, you go and get a Coca Cola out of the cooler for me. I need to sit down and cool off for a minute."

Sol looked at her, concern in his expression. "You all right, Araminta? I never heard you stop before, much less want to sit on the porch."

She gazed over the pines at the disappearing speck. "I guess I'm getting old, Solomon. Particularly when I look out to admire the view and see a dad-burned mule flying over my store."

Solomon let the chair legs down to the porch without a sound. He stared after the speck, now gone out of sight, and nodded, his eyes blue as a spring sky.

"People think I'm a liar," he said, taking a sip from his Liar's Award mug. "And sometimes I do stretch the blanket a little bit. But in the main I base things on pure fact. It's not often that somebody as solid as you can see the evidence, though, Araminta. I take it kindly that you let me know."

Will Henry squinched his eyes, staring after the now invisible dot. He'd almost seen Slewfoot Sally's mule, himself. The animal seemed to know that Sol was still concerned for it, and maybe it came over often to reassure the old fellow.

A time would come when he'd see old Sam, plain and true. Maybe even...catch him? A flying mule—now there was a project fit for a group as good as his!

He glanced at Tim, dozing in the sun, his pop bottle tilting perilously in his hands. His gaze slid to Chuck, who was daydreaming, his eyes half closed. Les and Fane were devotedly sucking on their pop. A dandy crew. Just right for catching flying mules.

Solomon cleared his throat, and Will Henry looked up into those bright eyes. "I'd do the same," said Solomon Peat, "if I was about sixty years younger."

And he would have, too.